# THE DEPARTMENT OF UNNATURAL AFFAIRS

A NOVEL

BY ASHISH KUMAR SINGH

# <u>Disclaimer</u>

Firstly, I want to thank you for reaching this far in the book. I know how hard it is to get off your cellphone. This book is dedicated to the one person who asked me to stop writing it. Fuck you!! I am even planning a sequel.

Like everything in life, Adulteration is present in this book as well. If it was not evident, I have used AI image generation tools to create the opening illustrations for the chapters along with designing the book cover. I have also used grammar and prose correction tools to hide my lack of talent. I for one, welcome our AI overlords.

## 1

## **Toto, I've a feeling we're not in Kansas anymore!!**

"Tonight's the night…"

I whisper these words in the dark recesses of my mind as the auto rickshaw lurches along the nearly empty streets of Gurgaon. It is late—so late that even the city's neon glow seems to have given up on its duty—and I feel that familiar stirring inside me, that secret thrill and hunger that has never waned with the passing of centuries. My thoughts drift into a wild anticipation of what is to come, of a feast that promises the rich taste of fear and life. I remind myself that tonight, I have planned everything meticulously; the route, the isolation, and the perfect opportunity to indulge in my most primal desires.

I sit in silence as the rickshaw's engine drones steadily. Outside, the world is hushed; only a few stray lights and the distant murmur of late-night traffic accompany my journey. I close my eyes for a moment, lost in recollections of distant, glorious nights—nights when my kind roamed freely and the thrill of the hunt was the only law. I picture scenes of past conquests, the pulse of life quickening before the final moment of surrender. Such memories leave a bittersweet smile on my lips, even as a darker part of me eagerly awaits tonight's potential.

Beside me, however, my companion on this journey is blissfully unaware of the storm raging in my mind. The auto rickshaw driver, a man with a lighthearted air, taps his fingers on the steering wheel while humming along to a slow Bollywood melody.

"Bhai, did you see Katrina's latest interview? I tell you, she's looking more dazzling than ever!" he exclaims with a grin that is miserably trying to light up his fat face. His incessant barking is chipping away at the focus of my darker musings. But alas, let him enjoy, for tonight's the night.

I had given him clear instructions: take the long, winding road to Golf course road—a stretch where the night is deep and solitude reigns supreme. Where there is no place he could escape to…..but I am certainly finding a lot of liquor establishments in the way….too many…wait there's another one. Nonetheless, this place is perfect. A place where I can finally be alone with the thrill of my intentions. Gurgaon, with its absolutely stunning crime rates and flickering infrastructure, is a perfect hunting ground for someone like me—a predator hidden among the sheep.

"Are you sure this is the right way?" he asks again in his annoying tone, I can see his eyes twinkling with innocent concern.

"And isn't it getting a bit chilly? Maybe we should stop for chai at that stall up ahead?" His voice, so full of mundane worries and pop culture chatter, makes my skin crawl with irritation. I force a tight-lipped smile, replying in a measured tone,

"Keep driving. Just follow the route I mentioned."

Internally, my mind seethes with impatience. I have far grander plans than listening to idle chatter about some mythical god named Sal Man Khan and his many heretic adventures.

Just as I begin to sink back into my dark thoughts—thoughts of the hunt and of a certain thrill that promises to quench an ancient hunger—a subtle shift occurs. The driver's easy demeanor gives way to a note of caution.

"Sir, I think there's a car following us," he says, glancing nervously over his shoulder. For a fleeting second, a flicker of irritation crosses my mind. Could it be that he has begun to suspect something is amiss? I dismiss his concern with a cool murmur.

"It's nothing. Just another vehicle on the road. Keep going." Even as I say it, I sense his stupid determination to ensure my safety, though he knows nothing of the hidden nature behind my calm facade.

Before long, the rickshaw slows to a halt. Behind us, also stopping at a distance and on the opposite side of the road, is a small car with a local number plate. I watch through the narrow window as the driver steps out, his steps steady but alert, and walks purposefully toward the halted car. My carefully laid plans, already on the cusp of fruition, are getting interrupted by this unexpected turn. I sit silently, seething with irritation at the delay.

I strain my eyes in the dim light and see that inside the car are two figures. One appears to be of average height, his features set in an expression that is both cautious and curious; the other is a larger man wearing a turban, whose presence seems to carry an inexplicable weight. They do not strike me as overt threats, yet there is something in the air— something powerful and strangely unnatural—that pricks at my awareness. I sense, almost imperceptibly, a presence that does not belong to the usual flow of the world.

After a few moments, the driver returns to the rickshaw. He leans out, his tone a mix of bemusement and duty.

"Sir, these two want to talk to you. They're saying you're… some sort of demon," he announces casually, as though it were a remark meant for banter rather than a challenge.

I feel a spark of anger kindle within me at the crude label, though I do not let it show. Demon—such a word is far too crude for the intricacies of what I truly am, but it stings all the same.

I step out of the rickshaw. My steps are silent on the cool pavement as I approach the small car, my mind reeling with thoughts both ancient and dark. I am annoyed and frustrated. Under the weak glow of a solitary streetlamp, the two figures come into clearer view. The shorter man, fixes his eyes upon me. Beside him stands the large, turbaned man. Their expressions are unreadable, and though I sense no overt hostility, I should just bribe them and get them going. Tonight, I don't want any interruption.

"Who are you?" I demand, my voice low and concealing my anger.

"And how much money do you need to get the hell out of here?" Bribing is not something is within my dignity, my pride refuses it. My unyielding pride—a pride born of a past filled with battles and conquests.

The shorter guy speaks first, his words clipped and official.

"We work with the government. We have noticed your unusual presence in the city, and you are required to come with us for questioning. There is no need for hostility…if you cooperate." His voice flat and monotonous, delivered in a tone that makes it sound like a line from an official report rather than a threat.

I scoff inwardly. Threats and bureaucratic orders mean nothing to me. I have known far more brutal eras, where the language of conquest was measured in deeds rather than words. I did not want to do this but three are better than one. In a surge of dark, instinctive fury, I lunge forward, intent on silencing him with the raw force of my anger. But as I rush toward him, an unexpected chill grips my limbs—a sensation like invisible bonds wrapping around my hands and feet. I falter, momentarily surprised by the restraint that stops my assault in its tracks.

For an agonizing moment, I struggle against these unseen chains—chains that seem to be made of nothing but the night itself. There is someone else here as well. I summon every ounce of my strength, drawing on ancient reserves, and I break free. In that split second, I launch myself once more toward the younger one, but he steps aside at the last second. He knows. Before I can continue, the spectral restraints tighten again, and I find myself caught in a struggle I did not foresee.

Amid the chaos, the larger man—barks a command at the younger one:

"Throw the solution!"

His voice booms through the night, and before I can fully comprehend his words, I see the younger one rifling through his pockets in exasperation, searching for something he calls "the solution." In the ensuing confusion, a crushing blow lands on my jaw—a punch so forceful that I collapse onto the cold pavement, my body suddenly heavy and unresponsive. These people are not who they look like. They know who I am, and they have come prepared.

I lie there, the taste of humiliation mingling on my tongue, as I struggle to rise. My vision swims, and the world around me blurs into a haze of dim streetlights and shouts. The big one moves closer, brandishing a strange contraption that appears to be a face restraint paired with a set of special cuffs. I need to get out of here, I need to muster the strength to fight back. This cannot be it.

"Yaah!!!" The auto rickshaw driver, leaps into the fray. He climbs atop the large person with determined haste, the fool is useful after all.

"Bhai, get off! This is dangerous!" cries out the smaller man, his voice edged with genuine concern.

I can only hear the commotion as a cacophony of shouts and the pounding of my own blood red heart fills my ears. This is my chance. Summoning the remnants of my will, I force myself back to my feet. My body trembles with the pain of the blows, yet a stubborn, ancient fury burns within me. I need revenge. I leap once more towards the weaker one, intent on reasserting the dominance that has defined my endless nights. But before my attack can reach its mark, a sharp shout cuts through the tumult. The smaller man, his face set in determined focus, hurls a bottle-filled with a solution —directly at my face.

The liquid strikes me with an immediate, burning impact. I let out a guttural howl as searing heat explodes across my features. I can feel it: a raw, scorching burn where the solution splashes, leaving my skin swollen and streaked with fresh, hot blood. My limbs grow heavy, and once again I collapse onto the unforgiving pavement, the world spinning in a haze of agony and humiliation.

For a long, disoriented moment, I can see the rickshaw driver stands by me, his expression a mixture of shock and disbelief.

"What on earth is happening here?" he cries out.

The humiliation I am feeling is more than the searing pain surging through me. Taking advantage of my weakened state, the bigger one steps forward with a grim determination and pulls me up. With precise movements, he secures me by fastening those special cuffs around my arms and legs. Then, as if sealing my fate, he fits a cold face restraint over my battered features. I feel the metal press in, and a part of me seethes with the loss of control, while another part silently vows that I will never forget this humiliation.

They force me into the small car, the interior stark and the smell reeling of dead rats. Inside, the tumult gradually fades into an uneasy silence. My mind reels from the pain and shock; every breath is a struggle as I try to process the chaotic events. Outside, through the tinted windows, I hear the rickshaw driver's voice once more—confused and incredulous—asking, "What is going on here?"

"Forget this ever happened." it's the younger one.

"No way!" the driver says, I can sense a hint of excitement returning in his voice as he adds,

"I'm making an Instagram video of this—this is going viral!" His voice carrying a mixture of happiness and disbelief. If only I had my strength, I would have enjoyed video graphing my meeting with him.

The car begins to move, I lie there, struggling with my thoughts amidst the haze of pain and bitter humiliation. My face throbs where the burning liquid has left its mark, swollen and smeared with fresh blood. I am consumed by a dark mixture of rage and sorrow—a feeling that I have been robbed not only of the night's feast but of my pride.

In the silent confines of the moving car, I try to gather the scattered remnants of my thoughts. I recall the thrill of the hunt, the ancient promise of retribution that once drove me forward, and yet now I find myself trapped in a farcical modern nightmare. I have no understanding of these people who surround me, no inkling of their true purpose beyond the strange words they use. I only know that I have been subdued by forces I did not foresee, forces that remind me of a world I thought I had long transcended.

The ridiculousness of the moment, of my ancient pride being mocked by a simple, modern jest, sparks a flicker of…

"Shut up and keep quiet already!" the younger one booms. The command is as much a plea as it is an order.

My thoughts, a tangled web of ancient rage and modern absurdity, are left to simmer as the vehicle pulls away into the night.

"We can hear your murmuring you know!!" he says in a quiet tone.

I lie there in the back of the government car—my mind a storm of dark recollections, seething bloodlust, and bitter, ironic humor. Though I have been thwarted tonight, though I now bear the marks of modern contrivances upon my flesh, a silent promise burns within me. One day, I will reclaim this night, this power, and make those who dared to disrupt my feast pay dearly for their insolence.

In that moment, as the car drifts further away and the night grows even deeper, I cannot help but allow a small, ironic smile to cross my lips. Even in this modern farce—a world of bureaucracy, clumsy restraint, and viral videos—there is a strange humor that gnaws at the edges of despair. It is a humor that reminds me that even the most ancient of creatures must sometimes bow to the…

"SHUT THE HELL UP, the spirit can hear you and it is not at all happy by your unnecessary exposition. My Name's Devrat by the way".

# 2

## What a dump!!

I'm behind the wheel as we glide through the deserted streets of Gurgaon at nearly 3 AM. The car rattles along, its engine humming a tired tune that barely masks the ceaseless drizzle of red tape and outdated technology we call our lot. I hate this.

Beside me in the backseat, our catch of the night grumbles incessantly. His voice is low, filled with a venomous pride as he recalls days when he supposedly ruled a province in Bhutan back in the 1800s.

"Once, I commanded armies," he spits out between bitter threats, "and now look at me—tied up like a common criminal. I'll take care of both of you when I'm free!" His threats, laced with violent promises. I can't help but roll my eyes at his grandiosity.

"Keep it down," I say.

I'm already frustrated—my mind keeps drifting to thoughts I'd rather not dwell on: the girl I'm supposed to meet later, a potential match for my long pending marriage, and my car that's been giving me trouble for weeks. Repairs, paperwork, and endless bureaucracy seem to define existence these days. I don't care much for his ancient boasts;

I care for survival and, frankly, for getting this damned vehicle fixed.

Karandeep, ever the brighter spark in my gloomy existence, is sitting beside me. He's too busy checking his cellphone for cricket scores to pay much attention to our captive's endless ranting. Every now and then, he glances up with a grin, chimes in, "Hey, have you ever played any sports, mate? I reckon you'd be ace at cricket with all that old-school charm you're flaunting!"

His tone is light, carefree—a stark contrast me. How does he manage this?

I steal a glance at him in the rear-view mirror. Even as my mind broods over my own frustrations, I can't help but feel exasperated at the endless barrage of questions and boasts from our backseat guest.

"What exactly are you?" the captive demands in a tone that's as curious as it is contemptuous.

"How did you manage to capture me, anyway? Who are you people? I haven't been captured in the past sixty years"

I sigh inwardly. "We're government employees," I reply in a dry, matter-of-fact tone.

"Part of an organization that's been around for over a hundred years, if you can believe it. Our job is to keep the supernatural from disturbing the mortal world. Simple as that."

I can't help but let my frustration seep into the words—a subtle jab at the absurdity of our mission. To me, our work is a thankless burden, a constant grind through paperwork and endless red tape, where every case feels like a never-ending cycle of mediocrity.

Karandeep pipes in with his usual enthusiasm. "Yeah, we're the invisible hand that keeps things from going completely mad," he declares, eyes still glued to his phone.

"We've caught things you wouldn't believe, handled cases that would make your head spin. It's all in a night's work for us." He laughs lightly, how does he manage this? Is it drugs? Or the breakfast his wife cooks has some magical potion?

I shake my head in disbelief. "Invisible hand, sure," I mutter, not entirely convinced.

"But then why is it that every time one of your kind—beings like you—roams free, no one even bothers to notice? Our agency has been active for over a hundred years, and yet these ignorant beasts insult us daily." I say it with a bitter edge, thinking of how little respect our work seems to garner.

Karandeep snorts. "Maybe it's because our organization has a bad marketing team," he jokes, his tone light and teasing. "I mean, if you can't get your name out there, no one's going to pay attention to you."

He glances at me in the mirror, his eyes twinkling with mischief, and I can't help but let out a dry laugh despite myself.

"It's not really bad marketing to be honest," I counter, my voice low and weary.

"We deliberately keep a low profile. We want people to think we're nothing more than a myth—a conspiracy theory that exists solely in whispers and rumor. And frankly, it's worked for over a century." I pause, letting the irony of it all sink in. Our organization is so secretive that even we aren't entirely sure of its proper name.

The creature, his eyes narrowing with intrigue, leans forward and asks in a quiet, challenging tone, "So what is this organization called? What do you call yourselves?" His words hang in the air, a challenge to our carefully guarded secret.

I exchange a glance with Karandeep. "We're so secretive that we don't really have a name that everyone knows," I say, my tone dismissive.

"Some say we're the Directorate of the Unseen, others call us that other name you can't quite pronounce—but officially, it's all classified." I add this with a weary shake of my head, the words tasting of bitter irony.

Karandeep can't help but grin. "Actually, we do have a name," he teases. "It's just that the lower folks in the organization don't get to know it. Only the higher-ups do."

The captive listens intently, his expression unreadable. He continues, "And what else? How did you capture me? And what is all this about—these magical objects, the presence I felt or more like the presence I am currently feeling?" His question cuts deep, touching on subjects that are a constant reminder of our burdens.

I roll my eyes. "Shields," I mutter, the word carrying a weight of envy I'd rather not acknowledge.

"They're supposed to be protective spirits, guardians assigned to agents after a certain level of experience. They help guard against physical and spiritual harm—basically keeping our minds from shattering when things get too… intense." My tone is dry, laced with a mixture of resignation and bitter longing.

"Some of the employees have them—Karandeep's own shield is his grandfather".

The captive is visibly dumbstruck. "His grandfather?" he echoes, his tone laced with disbelief. "How is that even possible?"

I offer a mild, measured response, careful to maintain our secrecy. "Some things in this line of work are best left unexplained," I say softly, not really elaborating. My tone is flat—a guarded reply that reveals little more than the barest hint of truth.

"What about you", the creature asking exactly the question I was hoping it would avoid

"Well. Me? I haven't been chosen yet." I say it so flatly that even the captive seems taken aback by my admission.

Karandeep chuckles from the side, shaking his head. "Yeah, no spirit has really volunteered for you yet, Devrat," he teases, his tone warm with a friendly mockery that stings more than it should.

"Maybe one day, the magic will come to you." His optimism is infuriating in its persistence.

The conversation drifts, punctuated by the soft strains of a sad Bollywood song playing in the background—a song that seems to encapsulate the endless, wearisome cycle of our lives. I keep my eyes on the road, though I steal glances at the captive through the rear-view mirror. His curiosity is insatiable, and he continues to pepper us with questions about our organization, our methods, and our past conquests. I have to admit, the guy is politely curious.

"Tell me, how did you manage to capture me?" he asks, his tone laced with a strange mixture of respect and contempt.

"Your organization has been active for over a hundred years, yet I'm surprised our paths have never met? Surely, even a creature of my… nature would have caught your attention sooner." His words are as much a challenge as they are a genuine inquiry.

I snort in frustration. "We're not in the business of making headlines," I reply, my voice flat and heavy with disillusionment.

"Our work is meant to be secret. We operate in the shadows—quietly, deliberately—so that the world never knows how close it comes to chaos."

Karandeep, ever the lively one, chimes in with a laugh. "I mean, think about it—if we actually shouted about our exploits, the whole world would be running scared. And frankly, that would be too much hassle for us." He grins broadly, clearly enjoying the absurdity of our existence.

Throughout all this, the car swerves along the winding streets of Gurgaon, the soft strains of a sad Bollywood song playing in the background—a constant, mournful reminder of our endless nights on the job.

The captive, sensing that he's perhaps drawing too much on subjects he barely understands, falls silent for a moment.

I watch him with a mix of suspicion and annoyance, unwilling to let his questions disturb the monotony of our journey any further. From the rear-view mirror, I see him frown as if grappling with a truth he can't quite accept. I remain silent, my thoughts swirling in a morose haze as I drive on, lost in the perpetual cycle of duty and disillusionment.

Just as I am beginning to get annoyed, we reach out destination. I pull up into the parking lot in front of a decrepit government building which we call our office. I peer out the window, and my stomach sinks further. The building is nothing like I'd imagined I would be working someday—a ramshackle structure with peeling paint, a faded post office sign hanging precariously outside, and a courtyard where a few stray dogs laze about in the dim early morning light. It's hardly the imposing fortress of a secret agency you would envision; it's a relic, underfunded and unremarkable.

"This is where you work, isn't it? You managed to capture me, and this is the grand lair you call home. I'm insulted, truly." His tone is morose—a mixture of derision and resignation that I can't help but snort.

Karandeep grins broadly in response, his demeanor light. "Well, we are a government agency, after all," he replies with a shrug.

"We're severely underfunded, and this dump is as fancy as it gets."

We step out of the car and make our way to the back entrance. The night is cool and dark, with bulbs flickering intermittently along the walkway and a solitary street lamp fading in and out as if struggling to keep the darkness at bay. The atmosphere is heavy with the mundane and the eerie—a perfect reflection of our existence.

Suddenly, our captive halts abruptly. He stops and refuses to move further, his eyes darting to the shadows beyond the building. "I can sense… something…a presence," he mutters, his voice trembling with an emotion I can't quite decipher— fear, perhaps, or something akin to regret. "There's something out there."

I glance over at Karandeep, who, momentarily distracted from his cellphone, squints into the darkness. "It's probably nothing," he replies, though I can see uncertainty in his eyes. But our captive is insistent, his posture rigid as he peers into the gloom.

To the naked eye, there's only an old watchman sitting near the back of the building—a thin, withered figure hunched over a battered bench, his head bent as he reads from a tattered detective novel. The area is small, much like the front entrance but with a more austere, faded design. The watchman looks up slowly, his eyes meeting ours as if he's been expecting us.

He fixes his gaze on the captive and then turns to Karandeep, asking, "Are you the one for today?" His tone is measured, almost ritualistic. Karandeep nods without hesitation, a proud glint in his eye.

The watchman stands slowly, his joints creaking as he ambles toward an old register notepad on a rickety table near the entrance. He keeps his gaze fixed on our captive as he begins to note down something in a script that looks as ancient as the building itself. I stand back, watching the exchange with a mixture of suspicion and morose detachment. There's an eerie quality in the way the watchman works, as if the act of recording these details is part of some ritual as old as the organization itself.

All the while, the captive watches me with an expression that is hard to read—a mix of defiance and something akin to fear.

After a long moment, the watchman finishes his records and, with deliberate slowness, walks directly to the captive. From his pocket, he retrieves a small sticker embossed with a peculiar token—a symbol that pulses with a strange significance. With a measured gesture, he presses the sticker onto our captive's face. "You can take him inside now," the watchman declares in a voice that brooks no argument, his words carrying the finality of a sealed fate.

We exchange a look—Karandeep's face breaks into a satisfied smile, while I, for the briefest moment, allow a scowl to darken my features. I can't say I'm surprised by the ritual; it's just another absurd layer of our organization's protocols. With little more ado, Karandeep and I guide our captive into the building.

# 3

## Here's looking at you, kid

We walk into the office building—a relic frozen in time. The corridors echo with the shuffling of tired feet and the low drone of outdated fluorescent lights. The interior is unchanged for decades: peeling wallpaper, creaking floorboards, and a strong aroma of stale tea mixed with disrepair. I trudge along with Karandeep and our vampire guest a being whose ancient boasts and violent threats are as annoying as they are irrelevant. He's my fourth catch of the month and possibly the fifth vampire I have encountered (I am certainly ignoring the Vetala we caught in Dwarka, we had to let him go due to political reasons.)

The sparse few in the office barely glance up from their monotonous tasks. In the main hall, a man cradles a tiny cup of tea as if it were a chalice of eternal youth, while another is absorbed in reading a newspaper so old its headlines seem more tragic than current events. Off in one corner, a fellow watches television, his face slack with indifference. None of them spare a second's attention for our arrival.

Almost immediately, our captive's mood sours further. His voice drops to a conspiratorial growl as he surveys the gloomy interior. "There's something terribly wrong here," he mutters. "I feel… cursed, as though some malignant magic permeates these walls."

I can't resist a sardonic remark. "Cursed, is it? Perhaps it's just the ceiling leaking again," I say, dryly. "Maybe a bit of monoxide poisoning. This place has been around since the dark ages, after all—age really does get to you."

I make my way to the reception, a small desk cluttered with a battered logbook and a vintage telephone that rarely rings. I scribble my name into the register. The women at the reception lets out a sigh that sounds like a death rattle. Every entry is a reminder that I've been here too many nights.

Meanwhile, Karandeep ambles off toward one of the workstations. There, an elderly woman, fingers flying over a computer screen that likely runs on Windows 98, is deeply engrossed in her work. Her name is Deepti I think, they know each other well— her weathered face softens when he greets her in a low, conspiratorial tone.

After a few minutes, her eyes widen and, without warning, she shouts toward our captive, "Hey, do you know 'Gurech' from Bhutan?"

The captive instantly bristles. "Gurech? I know nothing of any Gurech!" he snaps, his pride flaring.

The old woman retorts, "He was captured just last month—a 300-year-old vampire from Bhutan!"

I roll my eyes so hard I can almost hear them. Our captive seems both outraged and confused. "I'm much older than that, and I don't know any such fellow," he growls.

As if on cue, his attention is snagged by something else—a red telephone mounted in the center of the hall, its color garish against the drab surroundings. The captive turns his head sharply and, in a soft, almost fearful tone, asks, "What is that thing?"

I push him forward, unwilling to entertain further his juvenile curiosities. "It's just an old phone".

"It hasn't rung in ages. Probably broken—just another relic like everything else here." My tone leaving no room for discussion, though I can't help but feel that even the mundane can seem mystical in this place.

Soon after, we lead the captive into a small, cramped cabin off to one side of the hall. Inside, a short, older South Indian woman sits, absorbed in a battered newspaper. She's the branch head—Anu, her eyes narrow in assessment as she looks up at us. After a moment of silence, she fixes her gaze on our captive and inquires sharply, "Did you cause any damage?"

I can't help myself from adding, "He did, apparently. Roughly 400 rupees' worth." My deadpan remark draws a slight smirk from Anu, though she quickly returns to business.

After firing off a few more clipped questions about his origins, his aim in the city, and whether he might be of any use to us, she turns to me. "Devrat, deposit him now," she orders. And so, with little ceremony, our captive is roughly pushed along, and we begin our descent via a creaking staircase that leads to the ground floor.

The atmosphere grows heavier with every step downward. The building feels more ancient here. The captive, still reeling from our earlier encounter, stops abruptly at a heavy door in the basement. His eyes widen, and he stammers, "How old is this place?"

"Older than 800 years, they say," I reply.

"This office was built on top of it. There used to be a temple here—at some point, that is. Now it's just another layer of government bureaucracy."

Just then, a fat, jovial man bursts from behind the door with unexpected cheer. "Devrat, my boy!" he exclaims, warmly greeting me as if we were old friends. Without much ado, he takes the captive's hand and guides him into the basement. "I'm in charge down here," he announces with a boastful grin. "I keep the detainees in their cells. You answer to me until you are extradited, mind you."

As if by routine, he adds, "Time works differently down here, so you won't notice it much." Our captive looks mortified, a mix of confusion and genuine fear in his eyes. I can't muster any sympathy—this is our lot, and there's nothing heroic about it.

I bid a curt farewell to our captive and ascend the stairs once again. I go to my desk—a small, cluttered corner that I begrudgingly call my workspace. I settle into a creaky chair, supposed to type up a report, but the fatigue and disinterest weigh me down. My mind drifts as I begin pondering and wondering how I ended up this place—I cracked the government exam and endured an interview that turned bizarre when I spotted a ghost in the corner. I remember that day all too vividly: I screamed, and the interviewer simply smiled, as if witnessing the arrival of a long-awaited miracle. I passed that interview, though I was assigned to this department—a department that, until that first ghost case, I'd known nothing about. My parents are proud of my government job, but they remain blissfully ignorant of the reality: endless paperwork, spiritual misfortunes, and the perpetual weight of mediocrity.

My thoughts are interrupted by the insistent chatter of Karandeep who comes up to my desk, he's the only guy here who I like here, but the friendship does come with some burdens, he begins to recount tales of his wife and kids. His optimism is a constant reminder of everything I feel I've lost—of the ambition that once burned bright in me but has now faded into a dull, monotonous routine.

Before long, Anu reappears, file in hand, and announces in a clipped tone that brooks no nonsense.

"We have a new case," she declares.

"There's a crime victim—a girl, about seven years old—recovered at a gruesome crime scene where everyone else is dead." She offers no further details; even she seems as unaware of the specifics as the rest of us.

"The name given is Poonam. Vamsi is bringing her in" She says

My curiosity is piqued, but a sense of alarm grows as I learn that Vamsi, was the first responder. This doesn't look like a normal assignment.

Vamsi, of course, is everything I'm not. We began our careers at the same time, but while I've been stuck in the mire of endless paperwork and existential despair, he's risen quickly—talented, efficient, and apparently far more adept in handling supernatural matters. He now sits with the special operations team at the Delhi office, a fact that gnaws at my pride with every passing day.

After the assignment is handed out, Karandeep and I retreat to the small lunch room—a cramped space lit by a single, flickering bulb. We sit at a battered table and have our food, it's our night lunch as we call it.

We start complaining about money issues, the relentless grind of our work, and the absurdity of our lives. Amid the drudgery, my phone buzzes—a message from the girl I'm supposed to be matched with. I answer politely, though my tone drips with disinterest. She asks some basic questions, but I have little hope. The match, like everything else in my life, feels destined to be as underwhelming as the rest.

Not long after, Karandeep's phone rings—sharp, insistent. "Vamsi's here," he announces with a mixture of irritation and dark amusement. We finish our food in silence and make our way back to the main office. As we step in, my stomach twists into a knot when I see Vamsi, smugly perched on my desk as if it were his throne. Adding to the surreal tableau, a quiet girl sits in a far corner with a fruity beverage in hand, her eyes cast downward as if she belongs to another world entirely.

Karandeep and I exchange a look—a silent, bitter acknowledgment of the rivalry that has haunted my career for as long as I can remember. We approach Vamsi, and he greets us with that haughty intelligence that I despise. With a casual, almost indifferent tone, he begins to recount details of the crime scene. "The girl was found in an apartment on the eighth floor," he says coolly. "There were six bodies—neighbors even mentioned bear-like creatures roaming about. Naturally, the police dismissed it as a wild rumor. I was sent to confirm, and I found her—hiding in a cabinet, crying like a child. She barely speaks, but I did feel some unusual spiritual fragments in the air." His words are clinical, precise—each detail delivered as if it were part of a routine report rather than a horrifying incident. After a few more facts, Vamsi stands abruptly and departs, leaving a trail of smug superiority in his wake.

I can't stand it. I make my way over to the quiet girl, feeling an inexplicable pull toward her. "Hey," I say softly, my tone tentative as I try to bridge the gap between my cynicism and whatever hope might still flicker within her. At first, she doesn't respond—her gaze remains distant and blank, as though locked in a private, unspoken sorrow. I mention something about cartoons—a shared, trivial interest—and slowly, I see a change. Her eyes brighten imperceptibly, and a few words slip from her lips, halting and uncertain. Our conversation begins tentatively, like the first few awkward notes of a forgotten melody. Karandeep sidles over and, with a generous grin, offers her some orange pieces from his lunch. The simple act seems to bring a flicker of color to her cheeks, though she remains reluctant to speak about the gruesome incident that brought her here.

Later, Karandeep and I retreat to a quiet room to ponder the strange placement of this girl in our office—why she isn't at a hospital or a police station, but rather, in the midst of our morose realm. We murmur among ourselves, our voices low and conspiratorial, when unexpectedly, she appears at the doorway. "What's with the red phone?" she asks, her tone plain and matter-of-fact as she points to a bright red telephone mounted in the middle of the office.

I feel a surge of disbelief and annoyance. "It's just a phone," I lie offhandedly, trying to sound casual. "It doesn't really work—it hasn't rung in ages." But the girl's eyes widen, and she states calmly, "The red phone is ringing right now."

# 4

## They're here!

When I first heard that red phone rang, I assumed someone in the IT department was pulling a prank. Or maybe a telemarketer discovered an unlisted government line. After all, in the entire time I'd worked at the Gurugram office—seven mind-numbing years of halfhearted paranormal investigations—that phone had never rung. A relic from older, more superstitious days, it sat near a dusty corner of the reception hall, a testament to the agency's lazy upkeep.

But this night, it blared like a siren, slicing through the usual hush of the office. People froze, tea mugs halfway to their lips, eyes transfixed on the red phone's flashing light.

I am with Karandeep in a cramped corner, half-listening to him gripe about our monthly budget cuts. Then we noticed the phone's shriek. We locked eyes, hearts hammering. Even the surliest staff members emerged from their cubicles to stare. The red phone wasn't supposed to ring. Ever.

Anu darted out of her cabin, face pale beneath the overhead fluorescents.

She barked, "Stay calm! We don't know what this means."

Of course, that only fanned everyone's panic. A few timid souls scurried away from the phone like it might bite.

I felt a spike of adrenaline. Without waiting, I crossed to the phone and snatched up the receiver. My coworker Ramesh, who usually spent the evening dozing at his desk, let out a small yelp as if expecting me to explode. I pressed it to my ear, ignoring my own racing heartbeat.

A raspy voice came through, sounding as though the speaker's throat was lined with razor blades. "They are coming. Escape."

Then a click.

Silence.

I lowered the receiver, goosebumps prickling my arms. "That was… unhelpful," I muttered.

Anu practically collided with me, demanding answers. When I relayed the cryptic warning, a nervous scoff rippled through the staff. Some insisted it was a prank. Others, including me, felt that knot in the gut that foretold something truly horrific.

---

The lone security guard—an older man who typically whiled away nights with endless chai— fidgeted restlessly, scanning the dimly lit parking lot through the tinted windows. Then he saw them. A small crowd of people drifting in from the far end of the deserted street. At first, he assumed they were lost travelers. But they kept coming, more and more of them, stepping from parked cars, striding with eerie synchronization.

The guard stood, adjusting his uniform. "Excuse me!" he called through the half-open door. "This is a restricted area."

A tall, hollow-eyed man at the front paused, cocking his head. "We're looking for a girl. She belongs to our family." He spoke in a flat monotone that made the guard's hair stand on end.

"Uh… I'll have to check inside," the guard managed. But alarm bells blared in his mind. Something about their faces—skin sallow, eyes dull—felt *wrong*. This was supposed to be a hidden agency building, warded to keep random strangers away. Yet these strangers walked right up.

He inched backward, intending to hit the alarm behind his desk. Before he could, one figure strolled right through the front entrance. A wave of impossibility hammered the guard—the wards should stop intruders. But it didn't.

"How did you get inside—?" he gasped.

The figure smiled with lips too dry. "I am neither mortal nor a spirit." Then, with a casual motion, he pulled out a knife.

Inside, I was trying to calm my own nerves. The tension from the phone call lingered like static in the air. People resumed half-hearted tasks or scrolled their phones, muttering that it must be a hoax.

Then I felt it: the building's wards. A subtle magical hum that typically protected us from random passersby. That hum flickered in my consciousness, like a heartbeat skipping. A hush fell as we all felt the wards fail in unison.

Something had broken through.

I swapped glances with Karandeep. In the corner, Poonam—the girl we'd rescued from a gruesome crime scene—sat near a table, sipping from a juice box. She noticed our tension, glancing up with wide eyes.

Before we could react, a thunderous roar reverberated from somewhere outside. My stomach twisted. The entire office froze, eyes snapping to the lobby doors.

We looked on in silence, until somebody stepped, and then another one, suddenly more and more people started pouring in. Their features were stiff, their eyes lifeless, yet they moved with grim purpose. They did not look alive to say the least, their flesh looks like it was decayed years ago, yet they looked entirely functional and aware. Some staffers screamed and backed away as half a dozen intruders strode into the corridor.

One of them, presumably the leader, intoned, "We want the girl. Give her to us, and we'll spare you."

The mention of a girl had me lunging into action. I dashed to Poonam, who stared at the intruders with confusion. "Stay behind me," I hissed, adrenaline pounding.

Karandeep advanced, fists clenched. "How did you get in?" he demanded. "This building is—"

The intruder's face curled in a mocking grin. "We have no time for threats. Where is the girl?"

A monstrous roar tore through the building from the back. I whirled around, heart pounding as I glimpsed a shape bounding in the corridor behind the staff lounge—a hulking beast, maybe bear-like or leonine, impossible to parse in the flickering lights. The entire office erupted in screaming. Even the undead looked spooked, glancing over their shoulders.

One of the undead repeated, "Girl. Where is she?"

Suddenly, as if waiting for the perfect moment, Poonam let out a tiny sneeze. The intruder jerked their heads toward our table. Reflex took over: I seized her arm and dove behind a desk.

Karandeep confronted the undead leader, face twisted with fury. "You can't just barge in—!" But the intruder shoved him aside, an inhuman strength sending him flying six feet into a row of file cabinets.

Pandemonium broke. More intruders rushed in from the front, and that monstrous, bear-like creature charged in from the side corridor, emitting a bloodcurdling snarl. People scattered, some climbing over desks, others sprinting to the staircase. The undead panicked as well, some turning to face the beast.

I didn't waste time. I grabbed Poonam's hand and sprinted. I knew where I had to go, the only place left where I could take a back escape. The basement.

We barreled down the stairs, half-stumbling as the overhead lights flickered. The beast's roars and the undead's guttural hisses echoed behind us. Heart hammering, I reached a locked metal door that led to the basement. I pounded on it. The guard inside, presumably half-asleep, answered in confusion, letting us in. The door slammed shut just as heavy thuds banged from the other side.

"They're coming," I gasped. "Lock it— now!"

The guard turned the key, shock etched on his face. "What's going on?"

"No time. We need a back exit."

He nodded, as if he has done it a thousand times, pointing to an older portion of the basement that opened onto a small loading area where his personal car was parked. Another dull thud rattled the door. These strange p were trying to break in. Fear spiked my veins, but a grim determination steadied me.

Then my gaze settled on our captive, the vampire sitting in the nearby cell. He too seems to be alarmed by what's happening upstairs. The creature glowered at us through iron bars, presumably mouthing some sort of obscenities in some foreign language I am not familiar with. A flash of a desperate plan formed in my mind: if we needed a distraction…

I rummaged for the cell key from a cabinet on the wall, ignoring the guard's protests. With Poonam clinging to my side, I unlocked the vampire's cage.

He emerged, eyes glinting with feral curiosity. "You have my gratitude," he intoned, only to be tackled *immediately* as the basement door buckled open under a savage blow. The undead poured in.

Chaos erupted, the vampire hissing as they overwhelmed him. While they wrestled, I seized Poonam's wrist, making a dash for the loading door. The guard fumbled for his car keys.

But just as we reached the battered exit, thud—the door was blocked by more intruders. They hammered the outside, presumably encircling us. We were cornered. Fear battered my chest. The vampire tried to fight them, but the undead battered him with unstoppable force. I glimpsed him pinned by three of them, hissing in surprise at their unnatural strength.

In a frantic move, I shouted to the guard, "Open the door anyway!" If we couldn't barge out, at least we might slip through. The guard complied, forcing it open a crack.

But a wave of undead arms wedged through, clawing for us. I reeled back, nearly toppling Poonam. Then, from behind, more of these freaks battered me, shouting in raspy voices, "Give us the girl!"

With a surge of adrenaline, I shoved Poonam forward, half-lifting her through the gap. "Run, get out!"

She stumbled outside, eyes wide, turning to call my name. Before she could pull me through, multiple undead latched onto my arms, yanking me back. The guard's shriek told me he'd started the car, but he was helpless to pry the undead off me.

In a final, desperate act, I shoved Poonam fully outside, slamming the door on myself in the process, effectively sealing my own fate. "Run!" I shouted.

Her tear-filled gaze was the last thing I saw before the undead tore me back inside, their rotten grips bruising my flesh.

They pinned me. My back slammed against a damp wall. The stench of decay nearly made me retch. One hissed, "The girl. Where is she going?"

I spat in fury, adrenaline throbbing. "You won't get her. You bastards."

A savage blow hammered my ribs, knocking the wind from me. Another undead pinned my arms, pressing me to the cold concrete. My mind whirled with frantic ideas: could I fight them off? Summon some leftover magic? But I was out of objects, out of options.

Pain exploded in my abdomen—a knife or some sharpened chunk of metal. The undead twisted it, gurgling a triumphant snarl. I gasped, numb shock flooding my brain. My vision blurred.

I felt a second, third thrust, each agony overshadowing the last. The world receded into a haze, my body sliding down the wall. The undead chattered about wanting the girl, but their words sounded distant, like an echo in a tunnel.

As darkness encroached, I ruminated on everything: the red phone that triggered this fiasco, the monstrous lion-like beast rampaging upstairs, the vampire I tried unleashing, poor Poonam sprinting away in terror. My final conscious thought was that I hoped she escaped. The Intruder's curses and shrieks mingled with the throbbing in my ears. My knees buckled. I slumped to the cold floor, vision tunneling.

One more stab lanced my side, and my world went black.

# 5

## It's alive! It's alive!

Devrat opened his eyes and found himself in a forest. For a few seconds, he simply stared at the towering sal trees, their branches interwoven like a natural cathedral overhead. A sultry wind rustled the broad leaves, stirring the heavy, humid air into a faint whisper against his skin. The smell of damp earth and moss filled his nostrils, alien and pungent. Confusion sank in; he was certain a moment ago he'd been lying in a hospital bed or possibly drifting in some half-dead dream state. Yet here he stood, balanced on uneven ground littered with old leaves and creepers.

He took one shaky step. The forest floor felt soft beneath his bare feet—wait, bare feet? Alarm flooded him as he realized he wasn't wearing the sneakers or battered loafers he normally did. Instead, his feet were clad in crude leather sandals, caked with mud. He glanced down, discovering clothes that were not his own: a coarse cotton dhoti, tattered at the edges, sweat-stained from the stifling heat.

"What the hell is going on?" he murmured. But the voice that escaped his lips was deeper than he remembered. Even the shape of his mouth, the resonance of his chest, felt off.

In the distance, he glimpsed a caravan of men, half-concealed by the massive trunks and thick undergrowth. They carried torches, bundles, and rolled-up cloth. Devrat felt an inexplicable tug, as though he was part of them, bound to their journey. So he walked forward, leaves crunching underfoot, heart pounding in uncertain anticipation.

As he drew closer, the men noticed him. Some wore turbans, others had long, unkempt hair. They spoke in low voices, occasionally glancing around as if searching for threats. He caught fragments of their conversation:

"Another month out here... I'm starting to think the King is chasing ghosts."

"He's determined to find that temple. We can't do anything but follow."

Devrat paused behind a broad sal tree. He felt compelled to speak, to greet them, yet he was terrified his voice would betray him. Then he spotted a small mirror propped against a cart. He edged toward it, dread pooling in his stomach.

The reflection that stared back was not Devrat. A middle-aged man with deep brown skin, a wiry build, and a thick moustache gazed wide-eyed in shock. His hair was unkempt, and faint lines of stress or exhaustion etched his brow. Devrat raised a hand to his face in astonishment, and the reflection did the same.

"This can't be real," he whispered, the phrase echoing in a voice far from his own.

A passing man—carrying a clay pot—glanced at him curiously. "You all right?" he asked in an Odia dialect. Devrat understood it, somehow, though he'd never studied the language.

"Fine," Devrat stammered, forcing the words out in the same dialect. The man gave a shrug and walked away.

Devrat realized he was seeing a vision. This is not his life, this is not his time.

Several hours later, Devrat found himself trudging along with the caravan. The forest canopy overhead blurred into monotonous green, the ground an unending tangle of roots and vines. Each step felt simultaneously real and dreamlike. He listened to the men's chatter: they spoke of a King leading them, a man of ambition who sought a rumored ancient temple in these wilds of Odisha.

From bits of conversation, Devrat gleaned that they'd been traveling months, losing men to fever, accidents, or sheer exhaustion. Yet the King pressed on, eyes gleaming with determination. They believed a god resided in this hidden temple, a deity that had chosen to linger in the mortal realm, granting boons to any devotee who found it. The King's obsession overshadowed the men's mounting fears.

At dusk, they made camp near a stream. Devrat's "body" felt worn, hips and shoulders aching from the day's march, hunger twisting his stomach. Some men whined about the King's mania, others shrugged that a mortal who sought a god might become more than human. One priest told a chilling story of temples that devoured their explorers. Another insisted the King's faith would lead them to greatness.

Devrat found the King at the center of the campsite, chatting quietly with a handful of priests around a makeshift fire. The King's eyes sparkled under the torchlight—a kind man with lofty dreams, but also an undercurrent of power-hungriness. Something about him radiated charismatic intensity. Devrat's borrowed identity bowed respectfully, feeling the pull of loyalty and caution.

"We'll press on," the King announced with a decisive wave. "No mortal achievements will suffice. I aim for something greater than flesh."

A murmur rippled through the men, some exchanging uneasy looks. Devrat felt a pang of sympathy, glimpsing both the King's drive and the fear it instilled.

Days and nights melted together in Devrat's unfolding vision. He, or rather the man he inhabited, endured harrowing challenges: fording rivers with raging currents, hacking through thorny undergrowth that left cuts on every exposed patch of skin, fending off wild animals at night. Some men succumbed to malaria or injuries from missteps on treacherous ground. Devrat felt the caravan's morale waver, the whispered doubts about the King's quest intensifying.

Yet the King refused to turn back. He believed the "god" in the temple was no mere legend—that to worship it was to unlock divine power. Devrat's host shared these sentiments half-heartedly, though each day left him more convinced the expedition was doomed. The man's internal monologue seeped into Devrat's consciousness: We'll never find this temple. We'll die out here.

After many months, the ragtag caravan reached a clearing. Through the thick mist of dawn, Devrat beheld a massive stone structure. Vines clung to pillars carved with cryptic images. The caravan erupted in triumphant cries, disbelief mingling with joy. The King was overjoyed, face alight with the fervor of a man vindicated. The priests chanted blessings.

Devrat trudged up the overgrown steps, marveling at the scale. The temple soared overhead, older than any standard shrine. He noticed carvings that weren't of typical deities—not Vishnu or Shiva or any known pantheon. Instead, the walls depicted twisted forms, half-human, half-beast, or possibly insectoid. An uneasy hush fell over some of the men, suspecting demon worship.

The King dismissed their fears with a dismissive wave. "A god's true form might be beyond mortal comprehension," he said calmly. "Don't let the imagery deceive you."

Still, Devrat sensed the tension. Many whispered that this was no benevolent shrine but rather some demonic site built in archaic times. Yet the King pressed on, leading a small group of priests inside to explore. Camps were pitched in the temple's courtyard. Devrat's host, exhausted yet curious, helped set up tents, dividing supplies among the men.

Days stretched into a week. They scoured the temple. No typical idols graced the main halls, no treasure gleamed in hidden corners. Instead, they found creepy sculptures of insect-like figures: bulging eyes, chitinous limbs. Some altars were caked in dust, as though no worshipper had come for centuries. The King refused to let disappointment show, insisting they keep searching, certain the "god" resided deeper, or that they'd misread the temple's layout.

Others, especially the older caravan members, believed they'd stumbled upon a demon's lair. Devrat's host wavered between loyalty to the King's vision and a growing dread. At night, he dreamt of scuttling shapes in the corridors, echoing chirps that sounded suspiciously like insects.

On the third night of their stay, the King bolted awake, claiming he heard a voice in the temple calling him. With a handful of guards—Devrat's host among them—he ventured into a sealed basement chamber that had been overlooked. Dust choked the stairs, old beams straining overhead as they pried open a half-collapsed entrance.

Inside, by the light of flickering torches, they found a large insect—unlike any normal bug. Its exoskeleton shone with a golden finish, shimmering unnaturally in the gloom. About the size of a small cat, it crawled across the stone floor with unsettling grace. The King stopped short, torch flickering across his stunned features.

Devrat felt his host's skin crawl. The stonefly—or something akin to it—was impossibly big. Yet it radiated an eerie serenity. Instead of attacking or scuttling away, it simply roamed the dark corner, antennae twitching.

The King knelt, ignoring the guards' fearful warnings. He extended a hand. Devrat's host braced for a lunge, but the insect calmly let itself be picked up. The King cradled it, face aglow with triumph. "This," he whispered, "must be the god."

Some guards exchanged alarmed glances. The priests looked horrified. But the King had decided. He'd found his deity, or so he believed.

Within days, the King declared the expedition complete, ordering them to pack up. Many men were relieved—no gold, but at least they could leave the creepy temple behind. Yet the King insisted on taking the insect home. The priestly retinue balked, calling it an unholy creature. The King overruled them, too enthralled to let it go. Devrat's host felt a pang of unease, seeing how enthralled the King was.

They marched back across the jungles, the insect perched in a crude wooden cage. The King often released it in his own tent at night, speaking to it in hushed tones. Some nights, the guards heard weird chirping responses. Gossip spread that the King was going mad, that he believed the insect answered him telepathically. Yet no one dared speak out.

Back in the capital—some mid-sized domain in eastern India—the King made no secret of his prized find. He kept the insect in his quarters, talking to it at odd hours. Over time, rumors thickened: the King had begun feeding it drops of his own blood. Devrat's host was present one fateful evening when a guard accidentally witnessed the King pressing a cut on his forearm to the insect's mandibles. The guard ran, pale with terror. The next day, the guard disappeared, and the King refused to speak of it.

As years rolled by, the insect remained alive—growing larger, to the point that it stood half the height of a man. The King aged, hair whitening, but the insect thrived in unnatural vigor. Devrat's host, occasionally on guard duty, glimpsed the King and his bug murmuring in half-lit chambers at midnight. He sensed no overt malevolence from the insect—only an unnerving presence.

Then the King introduced the insect to the royal court during the coronation of his young son. By then, the insect's form had changed: elongated limbs, a more complex exoskeleton reminiscent of partial humanoid shape. The courtiers gasped. Some thought it was an abomination, others wondered if it was a divine sign. The King beamed with pride. Over the following years, father and son spent evenings conversing with it behind closed doors,

When the King lay on his deathbed, the insect remained by his side, refusing to leave. He died peacefully, a satisfied smile on his lips. The new King was torn, some ministers urging him to kill the creature and be free of its overshadowing presence. But out of respect for his father, he kept it. Meanwhile, the common folk gossiped that the insect was a demonic force ensuring the royal family's fortune—and punishing their enemies with subtle curses. The realm's influence soared as they overcame rival kingdoms with uncanny ease. Many attributed it to the insect's hidden power, others to normal political strategy.

Devrat witnessed generations pass in dreamlike rapidity. The insect changed further, appendages morphing to approximate a more human shape, though it retained an insectoid head, compound eyes, and chitinous plating. It even wore partial robes, conferred the courtesy of the court. By the fourth generation, it was upright, walking with near-human posture, letting out deep insect shrieks that some courtiers claimed to understand telepathically. The kingdom prospered, but a massive divide formed: many revered the insect as a boon, others despised it as a demon.

In another flicker of the vision, Devrat found himself seeing through the eyes of a younger court official, overhearing a whispered conversation between the family priest and a senior courtier. They argued that the insect was no god but an evil entity, an old legend describing a shapeshifting creature that "broke away from the cosmic order." The pair believed it was gradually brainwashing or guiding the royal family for its own ends, ensuring they never parted with it. They decided the kingdom had to be "freed" from its grasp, even if that meant killing the demon outright.

Devrat felt a surge of alarm. If the priests intended to kill this insect, what might that do to the family or the realm? The debate ended with them resolute: they'd gather supporters to "remove" the demon by any means.

As the conspirators parted ways, Devrat's vantage began to waver. A haze crept over his vision, the corridors swirling into shapeless color. He sensed his borrowed identity slipping away, replaced by the intangible emptiness of deep confusion. A headache pounded in his temples, bright light flaring like a thousands suns.

"No—hold on," Devrat mumbled, trying to anchor himself in the dream. Instead, the dream battered him with pulsing white brilliance. He felt himself jerk violently, as though someone had yanked him from the scene by force.

# 6

## I'm gonna come at you like a spider monkey!!

Devrat opened his eyes with a heaviness that felt like he'd been drugged. Everything was a hazy blur, as if he were peering through the bottom of a murky glass. Mild pain throbbed across his body, but it was oddly diffused; he couldn't pinpoint exactly where it hurt. He blinked, trying to will the world into focus. The ceiling overhead looked familiar in shape—flat, with overhead lighting—but it appeared bizarrely distant, as though someone had stretched the walls outward.

He moved his arms to push himself upright—except he couldn't feel arms the way he was used to. Instead, he felt these stumpy limbs that refused to articulate like human joints. Alarm spiked. His back twitched, as though his torso were balancing on all fours.

Something was definitely off about his body proportions. He blinked harder, forcing his vision to clear. A swirl of battered furniture, half-finished paintings, and stacked files emerged in the gloom, half-recognized from the Delhi agency office. The place looked bigger and more chaotic than usual, corners elongated, every desk or cabinet towering overhead like a monument.

His heart hammered.

"Where am I exactly?"

A slow, crawling realization seeped in that he was in some side room or cabin of the Delhi headquarters, but everything was wrong— magnified, as if he'd shrunk down to childlike scale. Worse, his limbs felt odd and contorted, lacking normal dexterity. Panic fluttered through him: had his soul ended up in some freakish shape again, the way near-death experiences had previously thrown him into bizarre visions?

He tried to speak, but the noise that spilled out of his mouth was a garbled yowl. That's not my voice. It sounded muffled, as though filtered through thick fur or cloth.

Before he could process, he heard a loud roar from the doorway, echoing against the battered walls. He whipped around, vision swirling. Karandeep loomed in the entrance, each step shaking the floor in Devrat's hyper-sensitized ears. The man's frame seemed massive, face too big by half.

"Oye! Devrat?"

Karandeep's voice blasted with the force of an amplifier, rattling Devrat's oversensitive ears.

"Can you hear me?"

Devrat tried to shout a reply—"Yes, stop yelling!"—but it emerged as a strangled hiss. Karandeep's expression twitched between worry and an almost comedic grin.

"Uh… sorry, sorry," Karandeep said, dropping his volume. Still, each word roared in Devrat's head. "Relax, buddy. You're safe. Sort of."

Safe? Devrat's mind reeled. He recalled the attack at the Gurugram office basement, that final moment throwing Poonam to safety. Then came knives, freakish hands dragging him, darkness closing in… He should be dead. Or comatose. Instead, he was stuck in a weird vantage, everything around him too large.

He tried to say, "What happened to me?" but all that came out was a pathetic whisper. Alarmed, he jerked away. Karandeep raised both palms, voice gentle. "Easy there, easy. Let me—uh—show you."

Karandeep stepped forward, overshadowing Devrat's vantage like a giant. With surprising care, he slid his arms underneath Devrat and lifted him. The sensation was jarring—he felt tiny, weightless, easily hoisted like a toy. That single thought made his blood run cold: a toy. Could it be…?

Karandeep carried him to a full-length mirror propped against a side wall. Devrat's eyes locked on the reflection. A big brown cat stared back, wide-eyed, muzzle parted in a startled hiss. Devrat saw the cat's lips move in sync with his own frantic exhalation.

He froze. That cat is me?

He let out a strangled yowl, trying to speak. The cat's mouth opened, revealing sharp teeth.

Karandeep winced in sympathy. "I know, it's insane. Just—let me explain."

Slowly, carefully, Karandeep set Devrat down on a battered table in the corner, mindful not to jostle him too much. Devrat steadied himself on four paws. The sensation of cat limbs was surreal—his sense of balance utterly different, tail swishing behind him.

"Alright," Karandeep began in a calmer tone, "you, uh, died in that basement fiasco. Or nearly so. We found your body. The time dilation down there was messing with your soul. Instead of decaying, it stayed… flipping between realms, I guess. The necro-division can't fully explain it. But eventually, they captured your soul before it vanished. Brought it here. Problem is, your body's too badly damaged to hold you right now—you'd just, well, die again from the pain. So they used an alternative host."

Devrat stared, ears flattening against his cat skull. The horrifying logic sank in. They'd stuffed his disembodied soul into a cat's body.

"Yes," Karandeep said softly, noticing Devrat's stunned expression. "The janitor's cat was a good subject—some small accident, I think. Perfectly fresh body. We couldn't find any human body in time. So, we used what we could. We revived you with minimal spells just enough to anchor your soul. Better than letting your spirit dissipate." He exhaled. "It's not an everyday practice, mind you— it's expensive and complicated. But your soul was in a weird, stable-limbo state, which made you a candidate."

A wave of mortification and fear churned in Devrat's chest—this can't be real. Then the memories: the undead stabbing him, the swirl of death. Indeed, it might be real.

"So I'm stuck… as a cat," he tried to say. That intention came out as a disgruntled whisper. Karandeep read his meaning in his eyes, apparently.

"Temporarily. Once your body recovers enough, the surgeons can reattach your soul. It's been done, though rarely. Usually they don't bother for regular employees, but the circumstances… plus you being unusually lucky with the basement's time distortion. You basically wouldn't decay."

Despite the terrifying predicament, Devrat felt a flicker of relief. He was alive, in some sense. Then gloom overshadowed it. "What about the Gurugram office? The intruders? Poonam?"

Karandeep set him down gently on the table. "Let's see. The undead mob killed six people. The biggest death toll we've had in seven years. People are calling it the largest fiasco since that Champions Trophy demon spawn incident. The entire country's on partial alert, though obviously the general public doesn't know details. The undead group vanished. The good news is, the girl survived. A guard managed to lead her out. She's here in Delhi, safe for now."

Relief coursed through Devrat's battered mind. So Poonam was alive. But six staffers dead, the largest tragedy he has ever seen here—this job never ceased to sting. With a resigned, defeated motion, Devrat lowered his furry cat-head onto his front paws. It felt soft.

"It's not all doom," Karandeep added, patting him lightly. "You get a second chance, once your body's stable. You're not the first soul reattached after near-death. Though, yeah, it's usually reserved for bigwigs, because it's so costly." He paused, letting the comedic irony hang: Devrat was no big shot, but the freakish basement fiasco had conferred him a unique pass. "In the meantime, you roam around as a cat."

Roam around as a cat. Devrat let out a long hiss-sigh, equal parts frustration and relief. So be it.

---

Over the next few hours, once the initial shock subsided, Devrat discovered he could move about with feline grace. Well, shaky grace at first, because walking on four paws and balancing a tail was weird. Yet the cat's reflexes and instincts guided him. He recognized the corridors of the Delhi office, larger than life, each door looming high. Staffers who typically ignored him or threw sarcastic jibes now paused to gawk at the big brown cat weaving between their legs.

Some recognized the glint in his eyes, hearing rumors of "Devrat's spirit is in the janitor's cat." More than one coworker gave him uncertain nods or half-waves. Others just found it weird to see a cat carrying a cellphone in its mouth. Because, yes, Devrat insisted on retrieving his phone. He needed a sense of normalcy.

He found Poonam in a side room set up for her—the agency's improvised safehouse. She was perched on a spare chair, nibbling on biscuits while flipping channels on a small TV. When he entered, phone clenched in his teeth, she turned and let out a small gasp. Immediately, her eyes lit with recognition.

"You're okay!" she cried, bounding over to hug the cat. Devrat tensed at first—I'm not used to being cuddled as a cat—but a wave of relief from her overcame him. She didn't recoil from the fur or find it terrifying. She was simply glad.

He meowed pointedly, dropping the phone at her feet. She blinked. "You want me to… read your messages?"

Another catlike nod. She picked up the phone, rummaging through his message apps. A flurry of texts from his mother, plus a half-dozen from the potential marriage match, popped up. Poonam turned to him with an amused grin. "Should I let them know you're still alive?"

Devrat tried to meow an affirmative, feeling bizarrely self-conscious. Poonam typed away, occasionally glancing at him for input. She sweetened his replies, turning Devrat's usual morose dryness into polite, borderline friendly responses. Devrat mentally cringed but also recognized it might be better than ignoring them.

Poonam teased him about how his mother wanted updates on the prospective bride, how the bride herself was texting worriedly about his well-being. Meanwhile, Devrat, a cat, hissed or meowed instructions that Poonam comically rephrased.

As if remembering something, Poonam gently stroked Devrat's fur, and asks in small voice, "How is it to die?"

A pang of sorrow coursed through him. He tried to reassure her in cat-sounds, half-lamenting that he didn't have a normal voice to explain. She gleaned enough from his soft mewls and head nudges to guess that it wasn't pleasant, but that she shouldn't fear it too much. The flicker of sadness in her eyes told him she carried guilt or confusion about the undead attack on her family.

Eventually, her shoulders slumped, and she confided, "My family was attacked by a mob like that. I remember them. They called themselves… something. But everyone in my family was a bad person." She said it without bitterness, just confusion, as though she couldn't align the reality of loved ones with the monstrous deeds she might have witnessed. Devrat felt a surge of protective empathy, brushing his cat's head against her arm.

Later that afternoon, Karandeep found him and whisked him away to a small conference room. Inside, a group of higher-ups gathered: Anu sat at the head of a battered desk, Vamsi leaned against the wall, plus three other senior staffers and, weirdly enough, a ghost with a faintly visible aura.

The ghost hovered near a corner, arms folded, presence flickering with an occasional crackle of ethereal energy.

When Devrat padded in, the entire group turned to stare. For a second, embarrassment flooded him, stuck in a cat's form in front of the agency's leadership. But he mustered his courage, bounding onto a chair with a small hop. Karandeep set an improvised translator device next to him—some magical doohickey that might help interpret his mews into approximate speech, though it was glitchy.

Anu raised an eyebrow. "So… Devrat. Care to elaborate on last night's fiasco?"

In a combination of hisses and the translator's stilted voice, Devrat recounted the attack, the undead infiltration, the monstrous creatures, and the glimpses of his vision about the demon-lion fiasco. Or as best as he could. The glitchy translator turned some words into nonsense, but they got the gist. Vamsi asked questions, scowling at the mention of corpses reanimated from a decade ago.

One of the staffers read off data about the two undead bodies captured. They were "unresponsive" once pinned; apparently the controlling souls fled. A rotting corpse from 10 years back shouldn't be moving at all. The group concluded that someone was using unknown curses or advanced necromancy to keep these souls from decaying, controlling them across bodies. That defied standard agency knowledge, since souls typically degrade or cross the barrier to heaven/hell—a barrier that's supposed to be unbreachable.

Anu tapped the desk. "So they want the girl. We can't let them have her, obviously."

A short agent grumbled, "We don't have the resources. Maybe we just hand her off or pass the case to the police."

Karandeep retorted, "Handing a demon-lion fiasco to normal cops? They'd be slaughtered. Or they'd deny everything."

Vamsi nodded, arms crossed. "We can't do that. We must keep her on the move, and find answers."

Anu sighed, glancing at the ghost, who said nothing but flickered with mild interest. "Alright. Let's form two teams. One checks the girl's original crime scene, see if there are clues. Another will contact the Odisha office, referencing Devrat's vision about an old temple. Maybe it's tied to these curses. Also, we found a suspicious vehicle left near the office— likely belonging to the undead. We track that too."

"I want in," Devrat tried to say, but it came out as a strangled mew. The translator turned it into "I… want… go." Vamsi gave him an amused look, half nodding.

Anu enumerated the plan: Karandeep plus two agents would investigate the suspicious vehicle. Devrat insisted on accompanying them despite his cat predicament. Poonam likewise demanded to come, apparently refusing to be left alone in a stifling safe room. Vamsi decided he'd tag along for his own side of the investigation.

"This could be risky," Anu warned. "But maybe traveling together keeps her safer, with more eyes on her."

The meeting ended with that resolution. Everyone filed out. The ghost vanished in a swirl of silent laughter, presumably returning to whatever dimension it hailed from. Karandeep gently picked up Devrat, heading for the exit. Vamsi escorted Poonam, who clutched a small backpack of snacks.

In the hallway, Poonam paused to cradle Devrat against her shoulder. Even in cat form, he could sense her relief that she wasn't left behind. She shot him a small grin, as if to say, "We're in this together." Karandeep pointed at the corridor leading to the parking lot. "Our car's waiting. Let's go."

As they marched out, Devrat caught a glimpse of his own human body lying on a gurney near the side of the hallway, medical staff fussing with tubes. The battered form—pallid, heavily bandaged—looked so alien, as if it belonged to a stranger. A pang of longing fluttered in his chest: that's me, or it would be…or it might not be.

## 7

**You've got to ask yourself one question: 'Do I feel lucky?' Well, do ya, punk?**

I've lost track of how many times I've sat in the back of a car, questioning my life choices—but this ride felt especially surreal. First, there was the simple fact that I was in a cat's body, perched on a threadbare seat of an ancient 2004 Toyota Qualis plastered with cricket and football stickers. Second, next to me was Poonam, a seven-year-old girl who'd survived a supernatural bloodbath. My vantage from the backseat was one of jumbled feet, chipped seatbacks, and the faint stench of stale samosas someone must have left here weeks ago.

Karandeep sat at the edge of the same bench seat, half-turned to talk with me and Poonam. Meanwhile, two other folks from the agency shared the front—an employee at the passenger side, and an older agent behind the wheel, the latter fussing at the battered gearshift. The Qualis rattled forward in a series of clanks, a far cry from modern vehicles. Outside, the sky hung low with the threat of late-afternoon gloom.

Ahead of us, a sleek, brand-new SUV glided with an air of superiority. Even from the battered vantage of our windshield, I could make out Vamsi at the driver's seat, his "special ops" team inside, one of them definitely armed. Karandeep grunted when he noticed my catlike eyes flicking to that second car. "Yeah," he muttered, "Vamsi's folks get better privileges. Guns, better vehicles, it's how the higher-ups do it. Meanwhile we're stuck in this battered jalopy with half-dead shock absorbers."

I wanted to snort—if cats could snort—but it probably came out as a muffled hiss. Six employees had died at the Gurugram office not long ago, courtesy of that undead assault. Tensions soared. The agency labeled it "Priority One," supposedly the highest emergency classification. But from bitter experience, I'd seen "priority" ring hollow. We rarely had the resources or staff to deal with lethal supernatural threats. "Priority one means nothing," I tried to say, though cat vocal cords made my voice more like a low growl. Karandeep, recognizing my tone, read my meaning.

He nodded, echoing my thoughts. "You said it, Devrat. Hell, the world could be ending, and they'd worry about fuel allowances or dear prices of amulets." One of the employees up front—an older man who obviously favored sports—gave a half-laugh, checking his phone. They all seemed to accept the bleak cynicism that came from working in an underfunded supernatural agency. Yet we trudged on.

We lurched onto a bigger road, picking up speed. Poonam fidgeted next to me, her seatbelt huge around her small frame. She stared out the dusty window, then turned to Karandeep. "Why are we going with them?" she asked, voice hushed. "Shouldn't I stay somewhere safe?"

One of the staffers in front pivoted to speak, confusion on his face. "Precisely. Why is the girl even here? She's a child, she belongs in protective custody or something. This is an active mission, no place for kids." He glanced at me—the cat—and shook his head as if I would offer some reassurance.

Karandeep cleared his throat. "Look, after the fiasco at Gurugram, these freaks might breach any location. Our offices are no fortress. This time we're with Vamsi's team, so if something hits us, they have actual weapons. Safer to keep Poonam with us than leave her behind for another infiltration." He offered a faint grin, hoping that logic soothed the staff's concerns.

Poonam nodded, though her eyes still reflected anxiety. The roads rattled beneath us. Our driver cursed at the battered steering, the Qualis's ancient engine roaring each time it shifted gears. Meanwhile, up front in the SUV, Vamsi led the way, occasionally signaling us with hazard lights whenever he prepared to turn. The modern brilliance of that vehicle mocked our old beast.

Karandeep leaned closer to Poonam, bridging the seat gap. "You asked about Vamsi, right? Let me fill you in," he began, voice rumbling in the cramped space. "He's the golden boy. Joined around the same time as Devrat—" he jerked a thumb at me, "—but soared up the ranks like a superstar. Within a year, he bonded with a protective spirit. People spend decades trying that, some never succeed."

My cat tail twitched, an involuntary sign of annoyance. I had no spirit. That stung, even more so because I'd tried multiple times to contact my ancestors' ghosts with no success. Meanwhile, Vamsi had snagged a top-tier spirit buddy in record time. Poonam blinked big eyes at Karandeep. "Protective spirit?"

"Yep," said Karandeep. "A ghost that merges with an agent, guarding them from nasty stuff. They can share powers—like telepathy, illusions, or direct spiritual blasts. A real lifesaver. But it's typically from your family's lineage or some volunteer spirit. Devrat here never found one." He cast me a sympathetic glance. "We guess his relatives had no interest in tethering themselves. Spirits usually decay if they don't bond with a host or artifact."

I let out a low hiss, the cat version of a sigh. Poonam gently patted my furry shoulder as if to console me. I appreciated the gesture, though it hammered home how humiliating cat existence was becoming. I tried not to brood too obviously. The conversation shifted as the staffer in the front seat asked where we were heading. "Any clue?"

Karandeep shrugged. "We follow Vamsi's lead. He found a lead about the undead's car or something. We'll see." He turned back, rummaging for a battered phone. "We're basically tagging along. The big boss has escalated things."

The driver piped up, changing topics: "Did anybody see the match last night? That final over was insane." He launched into a spirited discussion of cricket's finer points, analyzing how the bowler messed up or how the batsman slammed a six in the penultimate ball. Karandeep joined in occasionally, while the front passenger chimed in with football references. A wave of banter flooded the car—talk of goals, run rates, star players. The typical Indian sports fanaticism, or escapism, overshadowing the bleak supernatural day job.

I, on the other hand, felt a throbbing headache behind my cat eyes. The roar of the engine, the swirl of conversations—it all drowned me. I turned to the window, staring at passing crowds, dusty roads, and half-constructed buildings. My mind churned with heavier thoughts: how long would I remain a cat? The necro team insisted they'd reattach me to my battered human body eventually, but the procedure was complex, the cost enormous. And what if it never worked? My entire life might be spent as a stray in an ill-fitting job. Even if they succeeded, was this job worth it? We'd lost so many. My sense of purpose felt frayed, overshadowed by cynicism. Maybe I should just quit, leave this madness behind. But then, who would handle these horrors?

The car rattled on, the highway eventually tapering into a narrower road. I realized we'd left Delhi's outskirts. My whiskers twitched in confusion. We were supposed to head to Baraut to check out a suspicious vehicle linked to the undead. Instead, the SUV signaled a turn onto a secondary route leading somewhere near Rohtak, Haryana. I meowed questioningly at Karandeep, who also looked perplexed. "We're heading west," he muttered, "not east to Baraut."

We watched the SUV roll through a rural village. Vamsi occasionally stopped to talk with locals, presumably gleaning directions. Yellow mustard fields stretched on either side of the dusty lane, a golden wave under the late-day sun. The incongruity hammered home how surreal our job was: monstrous undead in the hush of farmland. After a half-hour of bumpy roads, we pulled up to a secluded cottage, small and nondescript, farmland all around.

Vamsi hopped out, marching over. "Karandeep, Devrat—get out. Bring Poonam." His clipped tone signaled urgency. We complied, though the staffers in the front seat exchanged uneasy glances. The modern SUV parked behind us, its armed occupant scanning the area. My cat body felt a jolt of tension. This place was remote enough to hide anything.

Karandeep opened the back door. Poonam slid out, clutching her small bag. I leapt after them, the rough ground jarring my paws. Vamsi beckoned us inside the cottage, explaining in hush tones, "We're here to see an associate—someone who might clarify last night's undead fiasco."

The house was old, the paint peeling, a single overhead bulb flickering in the front porch. We stepped into a musty living room. An elderly woman, probably in her eighties, perched in front of a small TV set playing a reality show. Vamsi offered her a polite nod and whispered a question. She jabbed a bony finger toward the kitchen. "He's in there," she said, voice raspy.

We followed, the floor creaking underfoot. Poonam hovered close to Karandeep, fear glimmering in her eyes. We turned a corner and stepped into a dim kitchen—and Poonam let out a shrill scream. My hackles rose, pupils flaring. In the far corner, a 7'5" bearded man with massive, curved horns protruding from his back was kneading dough on a wooden slab. One eye glowed red. He wore normal village clothes, old Bollywood tunes crackling from a cheap radio. The entire image defied logic, especially the horns and monstrous height.

Startled by the scream, the man turned. His broad, scarred face broke into a sad smile when he spotted Vamsi. "You again. Been a while," he said in a deep, melodic baritone. He glanced at the rest of us—the cat (me), Karandeep, and the trembling Poonam. "What's all this?"

Vamsi approached calmly, exchanging pleasantries as if reuniting with an old friend. They chatted briefly about local news, the fields, the dryness of the region. Meanwhile, I edged behind a battered stool. Karandeep leaned down to me, whispering, "He's a demon. Some choose to remain in the mortal realm, giving up big ambitions. We let them be. This one's named Chedipe." Then he corrected himself, "He calls himself Chirayu these days."

So the demon was a docile retiree living in farmland. Because of course that existed. Poonam squeaked, inching closer. She nearly jumped when Chirayu set the dough aside and approached gently, eyes fixed on her. He took her hand with surprising delicacy, scanning her aura with a slow nod. "Yes, she has demon blood," he murmured, letting her hand go. "I can sense it. A faint presence from something beyond the mortal plane. Surprising."

Vamsi sighed, "Any idea which demon might've sired that line or how it spread? They can't typically procreate with mortals since the realms parted centuries ago."

Chirayu shrugged, horns swaying. "Should be impossible. The big barrier was sealed eons ago to stop crossbreeding. But here's evidence to the contrary." He flicked a glance at Poonam, who shrank under his gaze. "As for the undead fiasco, I know little. I sense a demonic influence at play. Possibly the same lineage controlling corpses for unknown aims. Some demon's bidding, no doubt."

Karandeep slid an anxious look at an old woman sitting by the threshold to the living room. He asked in a hushed tone, "What about her? Another demon?"

Chirayu huffed a soft laugh. "She's my wife. 567th wife, to be exact. She tolerates my horns because my cooking's good." The old woman offered us a weak smile, then returned her attention to the TV.

Chirayu turned to me—the cat—arching a brow. "Did you bring me a feline gift?" He smirked. "I appreciate the gesture, but I prefer goat curry." My fur bristled. I meowed a protest, stepping behind Karandeep's ankles.

Vamsi cleared his throat, giving the demon a warning look. "He's an agent, ironically. The cat's just his body—for now."

The demon's eyes flashed with amusement. "Fascinating."

After a few more rounds of useless questions about last night's ambush, we gleaned nothing conclusive from Chirayu. He only repeated that a powerful demon might be orchestrating these undead folks. Possibly the same demon from which Poonam's lineage stems. Poonam's female lineage might hold special significance in the demonic realm. He couldn't confirm more. We left disappointed.

Outside, we clambered back into the Qualis. The sky had deepened to a dusky orange. Vamsi, standing by the driver's side, told us, "Now we can go check the actual location where the undead's car was found. Let's move."

Karandeep started the engine. As we pulled away, I overheard him speaking quietly to me. "Hey, Devrat, remember that second monstrous creature last night? The lion-like beast? Didn't it fight the undead? They seemed not allied but at odds. Maybe there are multiple demon factions."

I flicked my cat ears in agreement. "Yes." We both mulled over how complicated demon politics might be. In the front seat, the driver and the staffer still chatted about random nonsense, perhaps to keep from dwelling on the insane reality.

We caravanned onward, leaving farmland behind, merging onto a main road near Sonipat. At one point, Karandeep phoned Vamsi, suggesting we stop at a small public library he recalled in the area. Possibly they had reference books on old creatures or local demon-lore. Vamsi agreed. We parked outside a squat building with peeling paint, where a bored librarian let them rummage. They emerged half an hour later, arms laden with dusty tomes.

Returning to the Qualis, Karandeep told me, "We found something about lion-like shapeshifters. Maybe references to an older demon-lion deity that hunts undead. Not sure. We'll read on the drive." Meanwhile, I bemoaned the agency's archaic record-keeping—no electronic database to quickly search. We were stuck flipping through centuries-old volumes. The staffer driving the car snorted. "At least your library card's free. That's something."

The day crept onward. The sky bled into night. We eventually reached a residential area where that suspicious undead car had been spotted. Vamsi signaled us to stop some distance away, out of direct sight. The building soared multiple floors, lights in windows indicating families lived there. It looked heartbreakingly normal for a place that might harbor rotting corpses in disguise.

We quietly stepped out, leaving Poonam in the car with an agent to guard her. I hopped into a small shoulder bag Karandeep slung around, tail swishing in annoyance. "Better for infiltration," he whispered. "We can't waltz a cat around suspicious undead." Grudgingly, I complied, hooking my paws into the bag's edges.

We entered the building's foyer and found it bustling with kids playing cricket in a hallway, older folks sipping tea. The place smelled of homemade curries, the hum of normal life. My cat senses picked out laundry detergent from clothes drying on balconies. Hardly the lair of monsters, or so it seemed.

But as we climbed a corridor, weaving between the kids, I spotted three men among the group playing cricket. I recognized them instantly: the same freaks who had attacked us at the office. Their features were too similar to forget—hollow eyes, stony expressions, an odd stiffness in their posture. My heart hammered. I whispered from inside the bag to Karandeep, "That's them."

He stiffened, carefully passing the word to Vamsi via a discreet gesture. The plan formed: Vamsi would casually join the game, playing the unsuspecting newcomer, to get close. Then they'd quietly subdue them if possible. Another three agents hovered near, ready to pounce.

Vamsi strolled up, exuding a friendly air. "Mind if I bowl?" One of the attacker nodded warily, handing him the tennis ball. One or two onlookers snickered at Vamsi's stiff posture, but he forced a grin. For a minute, it went smoothly—he bowled, the undead battered the ball, feigned normal laughter. Then one recognized Karandeep lingering by the corridor. His eyes flared in alarm. He shouted at his companions.

Chaos erupted. The undead trio sprinted through the building's hallways, Vamsi hot on their heels, the rest of us giving chase. Doors slammed as confused residents peered out. I jostled in Karandeep's bag, hissing at each bounce. The chase wove up staircases, across breezeways. An older agent tried to intercept them but was nearly bowled over by a fleeing undead.

One of the undead launched himself out a third-floor apartment window in a desperation leap, landing with a sickening crack on the pavement outside. I glimpsed him through the window, legs broken, but he still dragged himself away. Another undead hijacked a parked car in the lot, squealing tires to make an escape. The third took a blow from an agent's improvised spear and collapsed, but then scuttled up, bleeding blackish gore. He managed to stumble out the building, eventually reaching that same car. They roared off.

However, we caught the one who jumped and crawled, lacking speed. Agents pinned him, forcibly restraining him with thick zip ties. He spat curses at Karandeep, at me (still hidden in the bag), but fell ominously silent upon spotting Poonam across the lot, wide-eyed in the other car. We shoved him into the back of our Qualis, muffling his mouth to keep him from biting.

Vamsi and a couple of staff rummaged the undead's apartment. They found IDs with contradictory birthdates—some men who should've been long dead, a stash of money from unknown sources. One undead was apparently "married," based on old documents. They seized passbooks showing suspiciously huge balances. The entire place reeked of necromantic anomalies.

With the captive undead moaning in the trunk, we decided to wrap up. We caravanned back toward Delhi headquarters. Night had fully descended, the highway lights flickering. Everyone was battered from the chase. Poonam was hungry, the staff exhausted. We collectively chose to stop at a Murthal dhaba—one of those roadside eateries famous for parathas.

# 8

## You're gonna need a bigger boat!

I've never been so grateful to smell stale lentils, sizzling onions, and a faint whiff of diesel. When you spend a day fleeing undead mobs, haggling with a demon over dough, even a rundown highway restaurant can feel like an oasis. It was late, the sky an inky black. Even the moon seemed halfhearted about shedding light on our predicament.

We parked our two cars: the rickety 2004 Toyota Qualis (my personal rolling coffin if you ask me) and the sleek black SUV that Vamsi and his "special ops" buddies commandeered. Both vehicles pulled into the gravelly parking lot near the restaurant's edge, away from the main building. When the engines died, the silence that followed felt almost eerie—no honking, no distant chatter, just the soft hiss of cooling engines and the oppressive hush of an empty highway at night.

Karandeep, cradling me in his arms like a reluctant house pet, climbed out of the Qualis. Poonam followed, clutching her little backpack and blinking at the dimly lit surroundings. Two other agents hopped out from the back, exchanging quick glances. One of them—the driver—hustled over to the second car, where I spotted the unconscious undead occupant slumped in the backseat, strapped like a prisoner from a budget horror flick. The plan was to leave two agents behind to guard him. If the guy woke up or turned feral, at least they'd be on hand to keep him from wandering off or snacking on unsuspecting bystanders. Because that's what we do, apparently—baby-sit undead detainees.

The rest of us trudged toward the restaurant entrance. The sign above the door flickered as if uncertain whether it wanted to remain lit, "Murthal Deluxe," half the letters half-dead. Just like us, I thought sardonically. Through the glass doors, I saw a mostly empty dining area—rows of plastic tables, a couple of bored-looking staff, and maybe a handful of customers scattered around. Hardly the bustling roadside dhaba you'd expect from the legendary "Murthal paratha stops."

We settled at a table near the corner, presumably to keep ourselves inconspicuous. Not that a grown man carrying a large cat, plus a quiet girl, plus an annoyingly calm officer was inconspicuous, but hey, we tried. Vamsi joined us at the same table— he insisted on it—while the other three agents sat at an adjacent one. I noticed how Vamsi positioned himself so he could keep an eye on the door. Old habits from special ops, I guessed.

The moment we sat, a waiter ambled over, looking half-asleep. "What will you have, sir?" he murmured. The watery overhead lights reflected on his balding scalp.

Karandeep and Vamsi shared a glance, quickly rattling off an order of stuffed parathas, dal fry, and an obscene amount of butter. Poonam requested a sweet lassi with an extra straw—some childlike indulgence that, for a second, made me envy her innocence. And me? Let's just say being a cat does wonders for your appetite. Or kills it, depending on your perspective. If I were human, I'd demand a double chai with an entire basket of parathas. But I found myself scowling at the thought of possibly lapping milk from a saucer like some cartoon stereotype.

As we waited for the food, Vamsi allowed himself a small grin—rare for the stoic golden boy. "We got one," he declared, leaning back in his chair. "Out of three, sure, but it's a start. We can interrogate him. Hopefully, that leads us to the others."

He glanced at me, or rather, at the cat version of me. If I had eyebrows, I would have lifted one. Instead, my tail flicked in annoyance. This entire day had been an endless parade of "we'll see what happens" from Vamsi.

Karandeep, meanwhile, flipped through an ancient, worn-out tome he'd brought from the library. He'd been obsessing about the lion-like beast that had crashed into the office during the first undead attack. The battered book had a Sanskrit title scrawled across the top, reminiscent of something that belonged in a dusty museum. I found myself craning my feline neck to see what he was looking at. The page featured a crude illustration of some monstrous creature, all fangs and fur and half-literate Sanskrit scrawl next to it.

"You understand that script?" I asked, or tried to. It emerged as a half-meow, half-grumble, but Karandeep got the gist. He spared me a sideways glance, answering in his usual conspiratorial tone.

"They gave me a Sanskrit crash course last year, when we had to decipher old temple writings. It's not perfect, but I can manage." He traced a finger across the lines, muttering a few words under his breath. "This beast… it might be connected to the same cluster of anomalies we faced. If I can find the right passage, maybe we'll figure out a name or a weakness."

I flicked an ear. Weakness, yes that would be nice. Because so far, the agency had displayed all the cunning of a headless chicken in dealing with these unstoppable creatures. If we didn't find a clue soon, we might as well resign ourselves to picking up leftover bits of undead in back alleys for the rest of our shortened lives.

Poonam nudged Karandeep. "He's got more messages from the potential match," she said, holding up my phone. My phone. The same phone I couldn't operate with these stupid paws. I hissed softly in protest, but Poonam gave me a wry smile. "Should I type back?"

I was half-tempted to ignore the girl's texts. After all, a single undead fiasco was enough to ruin any attempt at normalcy. But Poonam insisted, and there was something in her eyes—a gentle, concerned glimmer—that made me relent. So, we orchestrated a bizarre system: I would meow my general sentiments (or so I tried), and Poonam would paraphrase them into actual text. Of course, she took creative liberties, turning my sarcastic complaints into some cheerful banter. The entire ordeal felt like pantomime—my muzzle opening for a hiss, her giggling as she typed out some cutesy response.

"I can't do this job and maintain a normal relationship," I tried to tell her, which presumably she interpreted as me huffing with resignation. She typed something, then read it back: "Hi, how are you? Great day so far, just traveling around for official work." Great day? Official work? If I had eyebrows, they'd have disappeared into my hairline. The situation was so far from "great" that I nearly choked on my own cat-spit.

Still, the mismatch ironically made me reflect on how impossible normal life was for me. Even before turning into a cat, I was an agent in a secret government department that handled undead, demons, and cosmic horrors. Not exactly the kind of job that lends itself to stable romantic dinners or weekend getaways. And now, with undead on the loose, a partially demon girl depending on us, and a hole in my chest from where I was stabbed, I doubted any normal person would put up with me.

Poonam sensed my gloom. She patted my head gently, offering a small smile. "You know, you're not as grumpy as you think," she said softly.

I let out a halfhearted hiss-laugh. I wanted to protest that yes, I was exactly that grumpy, but cat vocal cords weren't designed for nuanced arguments. Instead, I settled for staring at her with a look that hopefully conveyed "You don't know how messed up this job is." If she read my expression, she didn't show it. She just rubbed behind my ears, oddly comforting.

The food arrived soon after: plates of steaming parathas, huge dollops of butter, a metal jug of chilled lassi, some dal makhani with a swirl of cream on top. The aroma nearly made me forget my entire predicament. Even in a cat's body, or perhaps especially so, the smell of North Indian parathas was heavenly. For a few blissful moments, we all let ourselves indulge in the relative normalcy of a late dinner on a near-deserted highway.

Vamsi excused himself momentarily, presumably to check on the unconscious undead in the car. Or maybe to make a call. As he left, Karandeep and I idly chatted about family. He talked about his father's endless pride in having a "government servant" for a son, how his mother pestered him to get a more stable desk job, and how this assignment didn't exactly reassure them. Meanwhile, I meowed something about my own parents—nothing enthralling, just that they were proud I'd landed a government job, but had no idea about the undead or demon-lion fiascos. Poonam listened quietly, occasionally stroking my fur, her eyes flickering with a softness I found both comforting and unsettling.

Some of the other patrons in the restaurant glanced over at us, probably wondering why a big cat was perched at our table. One lady even took a short video on her phone, which only added to my sense of mild humiliation. But I was too exhausted to care. After all, how many days had it been since I'd last had a moment to breathe?

Suddenly, Vamsi burst back into the restaurant. His usually stoic face looked rattled. "He's awake," he said breathlessly. "The undead. He's... conscious."

Karandeep set down his paratha, wiping his hands on a napkin. "We'd better see if he'll talk."

Poonam, presumably uneasy about meeting the half-dead occupant, stayed behind. "I'll keep an eye on the table," she murmured, though a flicker of fear shadowed her eyes. Devrat meowed, half wanting to stay with her, half curious to hear what the undead would say. Ultimately, Vamsi grabbed me by the scruff and lifted me gently. "Come on, cat agent," he said with the faintest smirk, and marched us back outside.

The parking lot felt even darker now, with only a single flickering lamp casting an anemic glow. A hush had settled over the highway, no trucks or cars in sight, as if the entire world had gone to sleep. Devrat's enhanced cat-vision picked up details he'd have otherwise missed: a stray dog rummaging in trash near the corner, a cluster of moths battering themselves against a dusty bulb.

Two agents stood near the SUV, weapons drawn but pointed at the ground. The undead occupant had been trussed up in the back like a hog-tied captive, a complicated arrangement of ropes and zip ties. He blinked slowly, eyes rolling, as if adjusting to consciousness. Then, with a sudden sharpness, his gaze latched onto Vamsi. He opened his mouth, drew a breath, and spoke in a raspy voice that made Devrat's fur stand on end.

"Are you from the agency?"

Vamsi exchanged a glance with the other agents. "Yeah. You're lucky we haven't turned you to dust." No bravado, just a flat statement, as if discussing the weather.

The undead—male, short-cropped hair, half-rotten face—winced. "What… happened to the other two?" he croaked. "Are they okay?"

A brief silence. Vamsi shrugged. "Two escaped. We only got you. Good for them, not so good for you." The man—thing—lurched a bit, testing his restraints, but to no avail. He let out a slow exhale, or something resembling a rattle.

He introduced himself as "Lipsit," which Vamsi remarked was an unusual name for this region. "Not unusual from where I come," Lipsit hissed. Then, with a twisted sort of grin, he demanded the location of the girl.

One of the agents leaned forward, eyebrows raised. "Why do you want her?"

Lipsit refused to elaborate. He only repeated that if the agency gave them the girl, they'd leave everyone alone. "We just want her," he rasped. A trickle of drool or some black fluid dribbled from the corner of his mouth.

Vamsi pressed further, but Lipsit clammed up, eyes rolling back as though he were losing steam. The body started trembling, words slurring. "Need… something…" he mumbled, then lost coherence. Within seconds, his entire undead form sagged, as if the spark animating him was flickering out.

Devrat hopped from Vamsi's lap onto the car seat, sniffing at the undead occupant with a mix of caution and revulsion. Lipsit smelled of decay, old dirt, and something faintly chemical. He mumbled curses in a half-dead language, then slumped once more into unconsciousness or perhaps something deeper.

Vamsi let out a frustrated sigh, telling the others to keep watch. "He's stable, but losing strength. We'll question him properly back at HQ." He then turned to Devrat with a half-quirked smile, as if expecting me to meow some brilliant plan. Instead, I hopped out of the SUV, deciding I'd rather not breathe that stale undead stench.

I padded around the parking area, half exploring, half needing air. The wide highway stretched beyond the meager lights of the dhaba, emptiness so profound it pressed on my cat-senses. The occasional wind carried the faint smell of farmland or distant factories. Then, something else. A different smell. Metallic, meaty, wrong. My fur prickled.

Drawn by cat-curiosity or agent-instinct, I slunk past a big SUV parked behind the main building. The smell intensified—rusty, like old blood. Another few steps, and I spotted a shadow crouched behind a stack of crates near a side entrance.

A monstrous shape. My heart hammered. The silhouette was all wrong—too large, elongated limbs, hunched back. Then, in the dim glow of a single flickering bulb, I caught a glimpse of it. Lion-like muzzle, thick fur, monstrous jaws. The same creature that had attacked the office? Or one of its kin? It was hunched over something, its mouth moving in a sickening crunch.

With a jolt, I realized it was feeding on a man's neck, presumably a dhaba employee. My cat body froze in horror. The creature turned, dropping the half-lifeless body, eyes locking on me with a predator's snarl. A string of drool or blood dripped from its jaw. Every cat instinct screamed RUN.

I did. The beast let out a guttural roar, launching itself forward with terrifying speed. I scrambled, claws scraping on the asphalt as I fled back toward the main building, heart pounding. A half-limp body—my body—sprinted awkwardly on four paws. The monstrous creature gave chase, bounding after me in heavy, earth-shaking strides.

I burst into the restaurant area, nearly slipping on the tile floor. A startled woman with two children shrieked as she saw me, or rather, as she saw the hulking monstrosity behind me. The beast roared, scattering plastic chairs, sending a stainless-steel water jug clattering across the floor. Pandemonium erupted.

Customers screamed, employees scrambled, some darted out the front door, and others jumped behind counters. Poonam spotted me barreling in and scooped me up, hugging me protectively. Karandeep was a second behind, grabbing Poonam's arm and pulling us both—cat included— toward the back, presumably to escape through the kitchen.

But just as we reached the door, we glimpsed another shape lurking among the cluttered kitchen counters. Another monstrous creature, perched among crates of vegetables, half crouched, silent. Twin glowing eyes fixated on us. A second lion-like abomination. So they traveled in pairs now. Great.

We recoiled, pivoting back to the main dining area. The first creature, hearing our frantic footsteps, whipped around from where it had pinned an unfortunate diner. Now it turned its fury on us, a deep snarl emanating from its chest.

Right on cue, Vamsi and two of his men burst through the shattered front doors in their battered Qualis, which they had apparently driven straight into the building. The vehicle slammed into the creature, sending it crashing into a wall. Vamsi leaned out the window, yelling, "Get in!"

Chaos reigned as Karandeep and Poonam hauled me into the back seat, the second creature snarling somewhere behind the counters. We heard it scuffle, presumably spooked or else disoriented by the crash. The engine roared, reversing with a screech, the battered Qualis now serving as a makeshift rescue wagon.

The other car was already outside, waiting. Agents waved frantically, yelling about the undead occupant or how the second creature might appear at any second. We didn't wait to find out. Both vehicles spun out of the parking lot, leaving the restaurant staff and any surviving patrons to piece together an explanation for what had just rampaged through their dinner.

Then, as we sped onto the highway, we saw them. Two monstrous shapes, illuminated in the rearview mirror, bounding after us with disturbing speed. Even behind glass, I could hear their guttural snarls echo in the night air, droplets of saliva or blood flinging off their jaws.

Vamsi cursed, rummaging for some magical artifact or another. One agent attempted to fling a powdered mixture from a bag out the window, chanting a half-learned incantation. The creatures didn't seem to care. They ran on all fours, or sometimes upright, either way moving with an uncanny loping gait that defied logic.

Time slowed to a panic-laced crawl. The highway was empty, no other headlights to be seen. One of the creatures tried to ram the second car, but ended up smashing into a passing truck that had emerged from an intersection. The impact was brutal; I glimpsed a flurry of fur, a roaring truck engine, then silence. The second creature, however, stayed on us.

It gained ground, howling with bestial rage, then leapt forward, hooking a massive paw through the open rear window of the lead SUV. Agents inside yelled, struggling to keep hold of the undead occupant. The monstrous beast gnashed its teeth, apparently determined to snatch the undead's half-limp body as if that was its prize.

From the battered Qualis, Karandeep hollered something about "cutting it loose." It took me a second to realize what he meant—he intended to sever the undead occupant's ties so the creature would be forced to take only that, leaving the rest of us free. The choice was grim, but desperation overcame moral quandaries.

Moments later, a horrifying sound of tearing metal and monstrous roars filled the air. The creature wrenched the undead occupant through the half-broken window, ignoring the shrieks of the agents trying to hold on. Karandeep hopped from the passenger seat to the SUV's open door, brandishing a short blade, and in one decisive motion, cut the ropes binding the occupant to the seat. The creature tumbled back with the undead body, smashing onto the asphalt in a swirl of dust and gore.

We pressed the accelerator, speeding away with a final shudder. In the side mirror, I caught a glimpse of the creature hunching over the motionless undead occupant, presumably retrieving what it had come for. Then the distance and the dark swallowed them.

A tense silence filled both cars as we finally slowed, the night once again eerily still except for our racing hearts. One agent exhaled a shaky breath, muttering a prayer in a language I didn't recognize. Poonam's arms around me shook slightly. I let out a low, comforting purr, or so I hoped. The entire ordeal had lasted maybe ten minutes, but it felt like an eternity.

After a few moments, Karandeep rummaged in his bag, retrieving the battered Sanskrit tome. He flipped to a page, showing it to the rest of us in the flickering overhead light. An illustration, stylized but unmistakably reminiscent of the lion-like beast that had just attacked us, stared back from the ancient paper.

"I think we found what's controlling them," Karandeep said, voice trembling but resolute. "Or at least something in that ballpark. This might be the demon causing all this mess."

Vamsi, pale from exertion, gave a grim nod. "We'll have to figure it out soon, or we won't survive the next encounter."

The rest of us, battered, exhausted, and riddled with confusion, could only agree. If these monstrous creatures roamed the highways, picking off living and undead alike for some demonic agenda, we had no choice but to confront them.

As the car sped into the darkness once more, leaving the shredded remains of a Murthal dhaba in our wake.

# 9

## There's no place like home.

I never thought I'd miss the claustrophobic corridors and perpetual filing-cabinet odor of our Delhi headquarters. But after the fiasco on the highway—two monstrous creatures and a near miss with an undead occupant, with the questionable comfort of an ancient Toyota Qualis—stepping back into the fluorescent-lit gloom of the agency felt almost like coming home.

Almost.

Through half-lidded eyes, I surveyed the chaos swirling around me. Agents scurried along the corridors, manila folders clutched to their chests like life vests, the dust motes under the ceiling lamps dancing around in lazy condemnation of the usual office meltdown. My body, newly reacquired from the cat fiasco, ached in every possible joint. Souls and bodies were never meant to be parted and reunited like borrowed library books. I was living proof that these emergency procedures might keep you alive, but they were about as pleasant as a root canal performed by an angry poltergeist.

As if to mock the seriousness of the situation, I noticed across the hallway—about four cabins down—a small group of employees celebrating a birthday. A couple of them even wore cheap plastic tiaras, while the birthday boy stood with a goofy grin, a half-eaten pastry in hand. They were singing an off-key rendition of "Baar Baar Din Ye Aaye," swaying in an awkward attempt at group festivity.

For a heartbeat, the difference between their cheerful celebration and the nightmarish meltdown we'd just survived made me dizzy. The office was always like this, some corners partying, some corners drowning in cosmic horror. I turned away from the spectacle, pushing open the door to a cramped meeting room that we'd commandeered. The overhead fan whirred with a metallic hum, and the single window displayed a smudged view of our alleged "secret" building nestled among BSNL and BSF offices.

Inside, I found Vamsi fiddling with his phone, Karandeep slumped in a battered swivel chair with a monstrous old Sanskrit tome on his lap, and two higher-up officials—Anu among them—who wore identical expressions of exhaustion. Another agent I didn't recognize scribbled notes on a whiteboard that squeaked in protest with every stroke of the marker.

I parked myself in a corner seat. My limbs felt like they were strapped to invisible sandbags. Even after returning to my body, I was still reeling from the "soul reattachment" fiasco. My body was mine again, sure, but it felt… different, like wearing a pair of shoes that had once fit perfectly but now rubbed in strange places.

Anu barged in a moment later, panting slightly as though she'd run up the stairs. She took in the room with a hawk's glare, then settled behind a rickety metal desk that served as the makeshift head of the meeting area. "Alright, talk to me," she said flatly. "You all look like corpses—pardon the pun. What happened out there?"

Karandeep flipped through the pages of his old tome, eyes flicking at me. I offered a weak nod— like, yeah, let's get this over with. Vamsi cleared his throat, leaning forward with that trademark stoic composure of his. "We had a lead on three undead targets. We captured one… partially. Then a monstrous creature attacked. Long story short, we lost the occupant because we had to cut it free from the creature's claws."

Anu's left eyebrow shot up. "So, you lost the guy."

Silence. Karandeep rubbed the bridge of his nose, clearly too drained to mince words. "We do have," he said carefully, "the occupant's arm. That… monstrous creature ended up pulling most of him away, but the arm got severed in the scuffle." He made a face that suggested none of us were particularly proud of that detail.

Vamsi nodded, a bit too eagerly. "Yes. With that arm, we could possibly do a DNA sequence or necro-analysis—maybe isolate some key markers to track the others."

The rest of us, Karandeep and me included, exchanged half-amused, half-disbelieving looks. The notion of performing advanced forensics in an agency that could barely afford new staplers was comedic gold.

Anu gave a dry snort. "DNA sequencing? On an undead arm? With what budget, Vamsi? You know how they are about spending beyond the usual. They'd make us file seventy forms just for an advanced dust test, never mind necro-forensics."

Vamsi's enthusiasm deflated like a pierced balloon. He set the undead arm theory aside with a shrug, mumbling something about how it was worth a shot.

Karandeep shut his tome with a dusty thump. "Anyway, we recovered other evidence from the undead folks' hideout—documents, passbooks, some random personal effects. We might glean a pattern or location from that. We can start sifting through it once we get an official clearance for a deeper search."

Anu nodded. "Do that. Also, I hear we have new findings on that demon courtesy of Karandeep. Possibly the same creature that attacked you at the office?"

Vamsi gestured for Karandeep to speak, but Karandeep waved me over. "Actually, Devrat can fill you in better. He was… partially there, at least in cat form, but he saw the beast up close."

I stiffened, still not used to talking about my cat experience as though it was a normal job anecdote. "Yeah," I said, my voice scratchy. "We suspect it's the same demon the basement time-dilation fiasco was referencing. Possibly controlling undead, or maybe they're working for it. The bigger twist is the girl—Poonam. She's apparently part demon."

Anu's eyes widened. "Part… demon?"

Vamsi folded his arms. "We suspect the demon is hunting her for reasons unknown. We also suspect the demon might have a direct link to these undead folks—like a necromantic puppeteer. But then, if that's true, why kill them or try to capture them? We're dealing with multiple layers here. Possibly a civil war among demon-kin, or undead sub-factions under demonic control."

One of the agents near the whiteboard piped up. "So the undead are also demons? Or part demon? Maybe they're a different bloodline? Or maybe the demon's controlling them to kill off rival bloodlines?"

Anu leaned back in her chair, letting out a long breath. "This is… complicated. We have a demon apparently targeting a part-demon girl, and we have undead minions who might be hunting or being hunted themselves. We need to consult the demon catalogs, see if we can find which entity is behind this. Possibly one of those old lineages we lost track of decades ago."

She grimaced. "But we're short on staff, short on funds, and short on patience. We'll do what we can. Meanwhile, we'll also see about checking the original crime scene where we found Poonam. Those corpses might have had demon blood. If that's so, this entire fiasco might be a demon feud… or something worse. I'd say we have about a week before the higher-ups decide to offload this entire case onto the police or some random other department."

The atmosphere in the room sank further. If the big bosses decided to pass the buck, we'd lose any chance of unraveling this madness. We'd also be leaving Poonam in a precarious situation if she was indeed at the center of a demonic power struggle.

Anu rubbed her eyes. "Anyway, enough for now. Meeting dismissed. Except… Devrat."

I froze. The memory of my newly reacquired body's fragility loomed. "Yes, ma'am?"

Anu's gaze pinned me. "Your body's ready," she said bluntly. "They cleaned it up. The cat's dead anyway, so no point letting you roam around as a half-crippled human. You can get a formal operation to reattach your soul now. Check yourself into the medical wing. That's an order. No sense having an agent who can barely walk or talk."

My mouth opened to protest—I'd only just stabilized from the basement cat fiasco, but the exhaustion weighed on me. She was right. I needed a real, official procedure to finalize my soul-body alignment. The impromptu method we used was about as stable as duct tape on a sinking ship.

Anu left the room, the group dispersing with her. Karandeep stepped up to me, raising an eyebrow. "Ready to go? The surgeons are waiting. Or… necromancers, or whatever the department calls them these days."

I nodded, feeling a swirl of dread and relief. This was my chance to truly reclaim my body, free from the half-limp feeling that kept haunting my every step.

Karandeep led me through a series of labyrinthine hallways. The overhead lights buzzed like bored insects. My legs still felt weak, though at least they were human legs, not cat paws. We reached a battered metal staircase—naturally, the elevator was out of service—and started climbing.

"How's it going to happen?" I asked, gripping the handrail so I wouldn't collapse. My lungs burned. Either the cat adventure or the soul displacement had shredded my stamina. Possibly both.

Karandeep shrugged. "No clue. This procedure hasn't been done in 25 years. Last time was for some bigshot politician who got possessed by a sea serpent in the Andaman's or something. Heard they locked the poor guy in a beach hut for two months with a specialized exorcist before surgically reattaching his soul."

I grimaced, imagining the kind of nightmares that scenario must have spawned. "Are we sure we want random surgeons poking around my soul again?"

Karandeep offered a weak grin. "Not like we have a choice. Also, we still don't fully understand how your soul stayed intact after the basement fiasco. Usually souls degrade or vanish if they remain unanchored for that long. That time dilation in the basement definitely played a role. Might want to keep an eye on side effects."

We reached the top floor, an area seldom used, where medical experiments or "nontraditional procedures" took place. The door squeaked open, revealing a small anteroom cluttered with half-functional monitors and dusty defibrillators. A flickering tube-light cast harsh shadows on the walls. Karandeep set me on a metal examination table, which squealed in protest. Two staffers turned from a corner TV set—they'd been watching some inane daily soap, apparently. Their eyes widened at my battered form.

A ghostly shape hovered in the corner, an androgynous specter with a pinched expression, presumably the head "spirit-surgeon." He glided forward, arms folded behind his back, wearing a faint glow like a ghostly lab coat. The staffers quickly turned off the TV, and the entire room went silent except for the hum of an overhead AC unit that probably needed a cleaning months ago.

I looked at my body—my real body—lying on a central gurney. It looked partially discolored, heavy stitching across the chest, evidence that the department had tried to fix the worst of the stabbing. My face was pallid, lips an unnatural grayish blue. My gut churned. So that's me? I was borderline corpse-chic.

The two staffers and the ghost simultaneously turned to Karandeep. One staffer, wearing ill-fitting scrubs, spoke up. "You can go. We'll handle it from here."

Karandeep gave me a small salute, concern in his eyes. "Good luck, buddy. See you on the other side." Then he slipped out, leaving me alone with the medical staff and the gliding specter, who stared at me as if I were a curious lab rat.

I tried to speak, but the ghost soared closer, pressing a frigid finger to my forehead. A jolt of cold shot through me. "This will be painful," it said in a voice reminiscent of wind over an open grave, "and the cat will die after the operation." If I wasn't half-dazed with exhaustion, I might have found a quip. Instead, I just managed a weak nod, unsettled by the ghost's final remark. Poor cat, used up for my sake. Guilt gnawed at me.

Before I could dwell on that, the spirit dug that ghostly finger deeper, murmuring, "Let's begin." The staffers donned gloves, stepping up with an array of half-magical, half-medical instruments. My vision swam as invisible forces yanked at me, pulling me out of my half-attached body. I felt a ripping pain, like a thousand needles burrowing under my skin, or perhaps under my soul if that made sense. The cat body, or what was left of it, receded from my consciousness in a swirl of dizziness.

My awareness flickered into a white space, blank and infinite, dotted with drifting hexagonal shapes and drifting orbs that glimmered in gentle arcs. I had no limbs here, no form, just a vague sense of being. Each passing second felt like a whispered eternity. Was this the fabled limbo between life and death, where spirits lingered?

The pain was there too, though muted, like a thousand dull knives pressed against me. I caught glimpses of the ghostly surgeon working, pulling intangible threads that must have been my essence. Then the shapes dissolved, and a new wave of agony hit. My mind reeled. Next thing I knew, the whiteness vanished, replaced by an oppressive heaviness in my arms, my legs. My body.

I blinked. The spirit stood before me, eyes vacant. "It is done," it said with unnerving calm. "You can live now."

I coughed, testing my new old lungs. My voice emerged as a ragged croak. "T… thanks?" A flicker of humor stirred in me, and I mumbled, "So, do you charge extra for this type of soul reattachment?"

The spirit didn't laugh, but a faint smile curved its transparent lips. "Eons ago, I did. Now, I only do it for the novelty. Humans rarely survive this procedure anyway."

My mouth twitched at that pleasant piece of trivia. "Neat."

Then I recalled the bizarre white space. "What was that place?"

The ghost cocked its head. "Between realms. A fraction of limbo near the barriers of life and death. Your agency tries to harness it for emergency repairs." Without further ado, it drifted backward, silent. The staffers closed in, presumably to finalize the physical end of the operation.

My eyes snapped open. I found myself lying on the gurney. The two staffers hovered over me, shining a small flashlight in my eyes, checking my pupils. My entire body felt like it had been run through a meat grinder, but at least it felt like mine again, no more cat limbs or half-limp nightmares.

"You can feel your legs?" one assistant asked, prodding my calf.

I hissed a bit at the contact—still raw from everything—but nodded. "Yes… sort of."

They shared a glance, then helped me into a wheelchair, hooking me up to a portable IV drip. I noticed the ghost had drifted to a far corner, perhaps bored or satisfied with its work.

By the time they rolled me out into the corridor, Anu, Karandeep, and half a dozen curious staffers had gathered, forming a small semi-circle. They gawked at me like I was some petri-dish miracle. Probably because I was. Even in a place that dealt with undead, demonic, or cosmic anomalies, soul reattachments were exceedingly rare.

"How do you feel?" Anu asked, pushing her glasses up her nose.

"Like I got hammered by a demon and had my soul reattached in a budget operating room," I croaked. "But alive, thanks."

Anu offered a short nod. "Good. You'll rest a few days. We'll handle the next steps."

Poonam peeked from behind Karandeep's shoulder. When she spotted me upright, in human form, her eyes lit up. She darted forward, gently grabbing my arm. A small, shy smile curved her lips. Maybe she was simply relieved that I was no longer cat-shaped. I mustered a faint grin in return, the wave of dizziness threatening to pull me under again.

Karandeep took hold of the wheelchair's handles. "I'll take him to his place. My block's not far from his, so it's easy to check on him. Let's go, buddy."

They rolled me into a waiting car—an official agency sedan this time, not the wretched Qualis. On the ride over, I asked Karandeep for a favor. He blinked in surprise but eventually nodded, heading back into the building for a few minutes before returning with a cardboard box. The weight of it in the trunk felt heavier than it had any right to be.

We arrived at my government flat, a modest space in a drab colony of identical buildings that never looked quite new or old, stuck in some bureaucratic limbo of dust and half-hearted upkeep. Karandeep maneuvered me up the elevator (miraculously working today), then set me on my feet inside my living room. My legs wobbled, but I managed to stay upright by clinging to the sofa.

"My wife will send food," Karandeep murmured, concern lining his face. "Take it easy. You just had a near-death and near-cat experience. Don't do anything insane, like chase undead on your own."

I let out a breathless laugh. "No promises."

Karandeep shot me a final grin, then slipped out. Left alone, the quiet of my apartment pressed in—a far cry from the day's chaos. I glanced at the mirror across the hall, limping toward it. My reflection was pale, a line of stitches crossing my torso, but it was me. No tail, no whiskers. Just a battered, tired man who'd had too many scrapes with forces beyond comprehension.

Weakly, I called my mother, bracing for a storm of questions. She was furious, demanding to know why I'd ignored her calls. I trotted out half-lies about "urgent fieldwork" and "unexpected lockdown at the office." She scolded me for a solid five minutes, then pivoted to the potential match she'd found. I mumbled something about texting her. My mother insisted the girl was wonderful, a perfect match. I made noncommittal noises, half my mind drifting to the cat fiasco. If only my mother knew I'd literally been a cat for a while.

Ending the call, I turned to the cardboard box in the corner. The cat's body, limp and lifeless, lay inside. Guilt churned in my stomach. That cat hadn't volunteered to host my soul. I owed it a respectful farewell, at least. I rummaged under my sink, grabbed a small spade I used for my neglected balcony plants, and hobbled downstairs to the tiny communal garden next to the building.

Night draped the sky, the dim colony lights illuminating patches of grass. I found a secluded spot near a half-dead bougainvillea bush and tried to dig a shallow grave. My arms trembled from fatigue. After a few attempts, I realized I lacked the strength. The cat's body deserved more than me haphazardly scraping dirt. Eventually, I set the spade aside, placed the box near the bush, and whispered a quick prayer of apology. Maybe tomorrow I'd get help burying it properly. For now, the best I could do was say thanks and sorry to a loyal cat that never asked for any of this.

Climbing back to my apartment, I discovered a tiffin box left at the door. Presumably Karandeep's wife, making good on the promise of nourishment. Inside, I found steaming rice, dal, and chapatis. My stomach growled in savage hunger. I wolfed it down while the news played softly on the TV. Some anchor was babbling about a "bull thrashing a Murthal restaurant." I chuckled darkly, suspecting the "bull" was actually the monstrous creature we had encountered. Official disclaimers rarely matched reality in our line of work.

By the time I finished eating, exhaustion overwhelmed me. My entire body felt as though it had been hammered into shape, not quite aligning with itself. Lethargy pressed on my eyes, luring me to bed. I tossed the empty tiffin on the side table, flicked off the TV, and collapsed onto my mattress. The springs squeaked like they, too, were complaining about my day.

Sleep claimed me fast. Too fast. One moment I was drifting, the next I was hurtled into the same kind of vivid vision-limbo that haunted me after my near-death. White spaces flickered, replaced by the sense of stepping into someone else's memories. Again, I was in a body that wasn't mine, seeing through eyes that belonged to some stranger, some figure from a century or more ago. A dimly lit room, nighttime. Flickering torches on stone walls. People huddled in a circle, their clothes old-fashioned—at least 100-150 years old by my guess. They spoke in hushed, urgent voices about a "creature" affecting the royal family. Anger and disgust laced their tones, references to "the demon that the king harbored" fueling their fear.

"We suspect the royal family is under its thrall," one voice spat. "It shrieks, they heed. They claim it's a boon from the gods, but it's only brought curses."

Another figure, presumably a woman in tattered garments, hissed, "It's demonic. The king protects it more than his own children. This kingdom rots under that beast's rule."

A younger man near the back spoke up, "They're traveling soon, meeting the British viceroy. The creature's traveling with them. That's our chance to corner it—kill it if we can."

The discussion rattled with tension. Some references to an "insect," some references to illusions. The entire conspiracy seemed set on ambushing the king, whose mind was apparently lost to the demon's manipulations. My dream-vision offered me no clarity on how this group planned to kill the unstoppable beast, but they readied themselves for a confrontation.

Then the night arrived. Through whoever's eyes I was borrowing, I witnessed them lying in wait, only to be discovered. Alarms raised. The king, furious, labeled them traitors. The group insisted they were saving the kingdom from "the demon that shrieks." One figure among them, heartbreakingly, was the king's own brother, who tried to reason with him. Tension soared. Soldiers brandished swords.

Suddenly, the beast appeared at the gate. As my vantage point fixated on it, I saw its shape, half-human, half-insect, cunning eyes brimming with malice, the once-chitinous limbs now disturbingly humanlike. A buzz-laced telepathic speech emanated from it, flooding everyone's mind with an unholy language. The group froze in horror. The king raved, calling the creature a "gift from the gods." The infiltration devolved into chaos.

The creature turned its head sharply. Its eyes locked onto me—**not** the dream host, but me. Devrat. A chill lanced through me. Before I could register the violation, the entire vision collapsed into swirling blackness.

I jolted awake in my bed, drenched in cold sweat. My heart hammered as if I'd run a marathon. The memory of that "insect demon" seeing me lingered in my mind, an afterimage that refused to fade. I scrambled for my phone on the nightstand, blindly tapping at the screen until I found Karandeep's number. When he answered, half-asleep and groggy, I barely managed to rasp out a few words:

"It's back," I said, my voice shaking.

He didn't need further elaboration.

## 10

### I'm surrounded by idiots

I'd always taken the Gurugram office's lazy hum of broken ceiling fans and mismatched file cabinets for granted, but walking back into it this time felt like stepping into the aftermath of a small war. The once-cluttered cubicles had been half-demolished by monstrous lion-like creatures, the main corridor was cordoned off with bright orange hazard tape, and the smell of disinfectant merged unpleasantly with charred wiring. A few determined souls in dusty coveralls were shuffling around with brooms and mops, trying to rescue the building from the latest wave of supernatural chaos that had battered it.

It was nearly seven in the morning by the time we arrived. Outside, the sun was smearing the sky with a faint orange bruise. Inside, the overhead lights flickered in that familiar ominous stutter. I found it oddly comforting, in a twisted way, to be back in the tattered remains of a place I could grudgingly call my home base. Part of me yearned for a normal nine-to-five job, but let's face it: if normalcy were an option, I wouldn't be dragging my battered body—and a host of cosmic nightmares—through a half-repaired government building on a weekday.

A hunched old woman, presumably hired on short notice to clean up the debris, was sweeping the corridor with an air of resigned exhaustion. She barely glanced at us as we passed, though I noticed her mumble something about "bloody demons" under her breath. Couldn't blame her. Even the custodial staff had learned the hard way that this agency didn't handle typical office drama.

In a makeshift meeting room near the back, I spotted Vamsi, Anu, Karandeep, and a few other folks—agents, mostly—crowded around a corner desk. The desk lamp shone a pale fluorescent glow across their weary faces. I slipped in as unobtrusively as possible and pulled up a chair that looked like it might give out if I shifted my weight too quickly. Over by the adjacent cabin, I could hear tinny music and sporadic laughter— somebody's birthday party, presumably. The irony of people dancing happily while the rest of us fought literal undead wasn't lost on me.

"You're late," Anu said, sparing me a quick glance before turning back to the conversation. She was scribbling notes on a yellow legal pad that had coffee stains from who knew when.

I tried not to sound too bitter. "Had to hobble a bit after reattaching my soul and all."

A few agents snickered quietly. Most of them were too engrossed in their own phones to pay me real attention, which was typical. Even after everything we'd been through, half the team was probably checking cricket scores or rummaging for demon jokes on social media. Only Karandeep and Vamsi seemed fully alert, their eyes flicking up as I settled in.

I coughed into my fist. "So… I guess we're debriefing about the fiasco with the demon-lion beasts, the undead occupant, and the highway chase?"

"That, and your dream," Karandeep prompted gently.

Right. The dream. Or vision. Or cosmic time-limbo fiasco. I felt my shoulders tense. "I'm not even sure how to describe it, but… after I got reattached to my body, I had another dream. Or vision. Like the ones from when I was a cat, but more vivid. I saw that same demon insect creature controlling a royal family, or messing with them, about a hundred to a hundred-fifty years ago. They were in some kind of confrontation with rebellious townsfolk who saw it as an abomination. Next thing I know, the demon was staring right at me, like it recognized me. Then I woke up."

Anu tapped her pen on the desk. "So we're supposed to believe your dream is a direct window into the demon's past. Or future?"

Vamsi gave a noncommittal shrug. "Temporal displacement is at least theoretically possible, given what he went through. He died, got his soul transferred multiple times, and presumably spent time in limbo. That might've connected him to…

well, something else. If his dreams are tapping into the demon's timeline, that could be an echo or an imprint. Or yeah, it could be random hallucinations from the stress."

Anu stared into space for a moment. "Even if we believe it, how does it help? We're chasing a demon that apparently influences families, spawns monstrous lion-like creatures, and uses undead minions. Great. Meanwhile, we barely have a functional staff. Our budget requests are a joke. The place is half destroyed. The higher-ups are breathing down my neck for 'tangible results' or they'll hand this case to the local police, who won't know the difference between a necromantic ritual and a traffic violation."

Karandeep leaned forward. "Based on the dream, maybe the demon's been messing with humans for centuries—particularly some royal lineage. It might have fathered children or half-demon heirs, one of whom is Poonam. So you have a demon bloodline out there, possibly waging war on itself. That explains the undead folks rampaging around, maybe. They're the demon's extended family, or they're possessed by spirits from that lineage. It's basically a very messy genealogical feud."

Anu let out a half-hearted chuckle. "So you're telling me the demon is actively murdering its own great-great-great-granddaughters? Sons? Nieces? I'm losing track. And we have zombies—" she paused, noticing a phone beep from an agent in the corner, who promptly resumed typing. She shook her head. "This is insane, but it's about par for our record, so I won't dismiss it outright."

One agent in the corner, a stocky fellow with dark circles under his eyes, rolled his shoulders. "What if the dream is just some leftover swirl in your brain? We can't plan an operation on the assumption that Devrat's hallucinations are accurate. Could be sabotage. Maybe some demon's feeding him illusions to lead us astray."

I bristled but tried to keep my tone calm. "I recognized certain architectural carvings. They're consistent with old palatial structures from the eighteenth or nineteenth century. Possibly in Odisha, or somewhere that style was prevalent. Did we get anything from that trip to Odisha we sent a team on?"

Anu shook her head. "No, not much. They're rummaging through old temple records. But you said your dream references a castle or fortress that might be three centuries old. Good luck finding that on a map. Could be anywhere. And I doubt local archives will have neat references to a demon's lair."

Vamsi cleared his throat. "We do have a small lead from the cut hand. Based on a standard necro-check and leftover identification, the body was once Ramesh Teotia, who died six years back in a car accident near Sonipat. There's a mortuary record for him, complete with a registration number for his remains."

A younger agent next to him brightened. "Yes, and from the documents we seized in that apartment, it looks like all three undead guys were employed at a logistics and transport consulting firm right here in the city. They were apparently holding down normal nine-to-five jobs. Hard to picture zombies working office hours, but hey, the economy is rough. Everyone needs money."

Karandeep cracked a grin. "Takes the phrase 'corpse-rate worker' to a new level, doesn't it?"

Anu gave him a look but didn't comment. "So basically, we have undead employees with real IDs. Except the IDs belong to people who died years ago. The spirits animating them might be from this demon lineage, or maybe they're random ghosts hired for a day job. Who knows."

I groaned inwardly at the complexity. Bureaucratic nightmares were one thing, but undead labor was a new high (or low). "If the occupant was literally a walking corpse, that means the real Ramesh was cremated or something, right? So how the hell did the body end up possessed for six years?"

Anu frowned. "We'll have to verify that at the mortuary records. Possibly the body was stolen or sold. Happens more often than we'd like to think. Great. Another errand."

"Let's investigate," she declared, ignoring the collective groan from the team. It was Saturday. Everyone wanted to go home and pretend their lives weren't overshadowed by demon genealogies. But the promise of overtime or the threat of demotion spurred them on.

Anu pointed at Karandeep and me. "You two, check the mortuary about this Ramesh. Verify the accident, see if there's a pattern. Vamsi, you said you want to check that logistics company?"

Vamsi nodded. "Yes, I'll handle that. Maybe talk to their HR or manager, see if anyone noticed three zombies shuffling in and out with coffee cups."

The meeting broke up with typical abruptness, leaving me stifling a yawn as I followed Karandeep out. My mind drifted to Poonam, who I knew was holed up in a temporary bunk in the Gurugram office. She was the center of this fiasco, yet nobody quite knew how to handle her presence. She had part-demon blood, undead relatives chasing her, a cosmic impetus swirling around. So naturally, the agency's solution was to give her a bedroom near the staff lounge, complete with old toys and leftover snacks. Perfect.

Before we left, I swung by her makeshift room. The place used to be a store closet, but someone had cleared the dusty shelves to fit a cot, a small TV, and piles of random goodies. She seemed content, munching on a packet of namkeen while flipping channels. When she saw me, her face lit up with a genuine smile that momentarily eased my stress.

I asked her if she was alright. She nodded, but I caught a flicker of sadness in her eyes. She opened up about how she'd lived a nomadic life with some joint family, never knowing her real parents or even if they existed. She recounted how they'd move from city to city, never settling, until that horrific night where everyone died, leaving her the lone survivor. I tried consoling her, though I felt pathetically unqualified. She had endured so much. If I was reeling from a day or two of cat embodiment, she had a lifetime of uncertainty behind her.

Eventually, Karandeep dragged me away from the talk, reminding me we had a job to do. We hopped into a nondescript sedan (slightly better than the battered Qualis, at least) and set off for Sonipat. However, Vamsi insisted on hitting the transport company's office first. Something about wanting to confirm details before we confronted the mortuary staff who might lie. Made sense in a twisted logic. We followed his lead.

Karandeep drove, all the while fiddling with his phone for cricket updates, occasionally letting out disgruntled huffs when the match scoreboard didn't go India's way. Meanwhile, I sat in the back with Vamsi, half-tuned to his presence. We rarely spoke on personal matters. But I found myself curious about his stoic approach to a job that was 90% cosmic headaches and 10% lethal boredom.

"So," I began awkwardly, "are you actually… satisfied with this job?"

He paused, a slight twitch in his brow. "It doesn't pay well, but it's something I'm good at. Also, I owe a lot to the teacher who guided me here."

He explained that he'd grown up in a remote Tamil Nadu village in abject poverty. A kindly teacher had spotted his potential, pushing him to study, and eventually guiding him to join the agency. That teacher was a former agent, apparently, and Vamsi discovered that the man's wife had been a spirit all along, living with them as though it were normal. The revelation that even his earliest role model dabbled in the supernatural didn't deter Vamsi; it cemented his belief that these intangible horrors had to be confronted by someone who actually cared.

I listened quietly. The petty envy I harbored toward his success dulled in the face of his earnest story. Here was a man who chose to be an agent not out of convenience, but genuine gratitude and moral purpose. Meanwhile, I had stumbled into the job chasing a stable government paycheck, only to end up in cosmic scrapes above my pay grade. Maybe that was the difference in our career arcs.

Soon, we arrived at the transport consulting office. The building sat on the outskirts of Delhi—a modern, four-story structure with tinted glass and a tacky metal sign featuring a stylized reindeer head. I recognized it from the ID documents we'd confiscated. The reindeer logo struck me as oddly out of place in India, but who was I to judge corporate branding?

We stepped inside. A bored receptionist fiddled with a thick manual about "driving trucks across state lines." She glanced up, unimpressed, as we introduced ourselves. Vamsi flashed a quick, forged identity from the agency's bottomless stash of illusions. The receptionist nodded blankly, directing us to the second floor, though her eyes flicked over us with mild suspicion.

We took the stairs, passing open-plan cubicles where men and women tapped away at computers. Some stared at us warily, but no one intervened. On the second floor, a man in his thirties with a wide smile greeted us. He introduced himself as Bijay Mohan Mohanty, a director of the company, flanked by two subordinates: one older, limping gent and a tall, thin fellow who stared at us with a gaze that reminded me of hungry vultures.

Bijay offered hearty handshakes. We reciprocated politely, even though the stares of his colleagues set off alarm bells in my mind. They led us into a glass-walled cabin—tastefully decorated, if a bit sterile— and Vamsi launched into an official inquiry about the three employees who matched the undead IDs we had. Bijay's face went from polite confusion to outright puzzlement as he studied the ID cards.

The thin man quietly took them to verify. Meanwhile, Bijay explained that the company had multiple branches dealing with logistics across states, including truck-driving services. He claimed not to recognize the employees personally but promised full cooperation. While he spoke, I couldn't help noticing how some of the staff outside occasionally looked up from their screens to eye us. The vibe was off, as though half the office was in on a secret we'd never be told.

The thin man returned, handing some documents to Bijay. He skimmed them, nodding gravely. "It seems these three are indeed on our payroll, or were, but they've been missing for four days. Two drivers, one coordinator. We have no further contact from them."

Vamsi pressed about the company's structure, any unusual happenings. Bijay insisted everything was normal. Meanwhile, Karandeep scrolled through his phone's pictures of the lion-like creature from the office attack, but kept them hidden. If the staff here were part of the demon's extended network, we didn't want to tip them off.

Eventually, we left with mild politeness, a stack of HR forms, and no real progress. As we walked back to the sedan, I noticed that same thin man at a second-floor window, watching us with unwavering intensity. A few other employees had stepped out onto a balcony, half-pretending to smoke while gazing at us. The entire building radiated suspicion.

The moment we were in the car, Vamsi exhaled, face grim. "They're hiding something. We'll cross-check these forms and see what turns up. Might have to do a covert stakeout."

We dropped Vamsi at the Delhi office so he could do "further analysis," whatever that meant. Then Karandeep and I set off for Sonipat, to find out how a body from six years ago ended up walking around as an undead minion for a demon-lion fiasco. Because apparently, that's our life now.

During the ride, I busied myself with my phone, searching references for the carving I'd glimpsed in my dream. My brain kept telling me I'd seen it somewhere in Delhi, but I couldn't place where. The same swirling pattern, half-lotus, half-solar motif, maybe some stylized insect wings. Or maybe I was mixing up two different illusions. The sense of déjà vu gnawed at me.

We arrived at the mortuary: a squat, depressing building that looked older than independence. Paint peeled off in thick strips, revealing a gray underbelly. A caretaker or mortician, a middle-aged man with nicotine-stained fingers, greeted us with the warmth of a drowned rat. He reeked of stale cigarettes and had a "no nonsense" scowl that suggested bribery would be needed to get any truth out of him.

He claimed to have records of the "Ramesh Teotia" body, which had arrived six years back after a fatal car accident. Registered, processed, and cremated, or so his dusty ledger said. Karandeep and I exchanged glances.

I tried to see if he was lying, pressing him with polite questions about how certain he was the body had been cremated. The mortician insisted, yes, he'd personally supervised the procedure. Of course, this flew in the face of our evidence: the guy's undead arm was literally in our possession not long ago. We called his bluff.

Karandeep stepped in, sliding the mortician a few bills. Then, in a low voice, threatened to punch him if he kept lying. The man hesitated, sweat beading on his brow, glancing around as though expecting a hidden camera. Finally, he broke, muttering that sometimes "certain bodies" were sold off for undisclosed reasons. He insisted it was victimless, as the families never knew.

We demanded records of such "sales," and with one last glare at Karandeep's fists, the mortician shuffled off to rummage in a locked cabinet. He returned with a stack of suspiciously unarchived documents listing bodies that disappeared into the black market. Sure enough, one matched the name "Ramesh Teotia," sold to an unnamed "buyer" for a modest sum. The same buyer had apparently acquired several other corpses, sometimes paying the mortician hush money.

We took that list, said a curt thanks, and left. The man looked half-relieved, half-terrified, probably expecting a crackdown or something. We had bigger fish to fry, though.

As we drove away from the mortuary, rattling over potholes and weaving through honking trucks, I delved deeper into my phone's search about the carving in my dream. Then, not far from the city center, something in my memory jolted me upright. "Stop the car!" I shouted at Karandeep.

He slammed the brakes, cursing, nearly causing a collision with a taxi behind us. Ignoring the taxi driver's furious honking, I scrambled out, scanning the street. My gut insisted something here was important. I saw a large sign for a heritage hotel, a sprawling old building with a refurbished facade. And its logo: the same swirling half-lotus, half-solar motif that haunted my dreams.

Karandeep pulled up next to me, shutting off the engine. "What the hell, man?"

I pointed at the sign. "That carving. The same design I saw in my vision. I'm sure of it."

The hotel did look venerable, its outer walls retaining some archaic architecture masked by modern touches. A few sleek cars were parked out front, presumably well-heeled guests enjoying some pseudo-royal environment. We strode inside, ignoring the doorman's half-hearted greeting. The interior combined ancient stone archways with new wooden paneling, the corners lit by warm lamps. A few staff members in crisp uniforms bustled about.

We didn't see anything obviously demonic. Just a normal, if somewhat grandiose, hotel. After wandering around the lobby, we ended up near the staff quarters at the back, hoping someone might know more about the logo's origin. Karandeep asked a few staff, who stared blankly or politely insisted they had no clue.

Then I pulled out my phone, showing them a photo of Poonam (I'd snapped one earlier so we could ask around). One of them hesitated, eyes darting to the hallway behind him, then quietly told us that a manager or part-owner might have recognized that girl. "He's in the rear staff block," the staffer whispered, "but I can't say more."

Intrigued, we followed the hallway to a small courtyard. An older man was there, barefoot, wringing out clothes on a makeshift clothesline. He wore a simple dhoti and a sweater that had seen better days. Thick glasses perched on his nose, and a greying beard gave him a dignified aura. He glanced up, curiosity flickering in his eyes as we approached. We introduced ourselves with the usual half-lie, half-routine about investigating local genealogies. The man introduced himself as Sarbeswar, from Odisha, a partial owner of this heritage hotel.

We showed him Poonam's picture. His face twitched with recognition, but he quickly masked it. He admitted that Poonam was his grandniece, had visited once, but the extended family parted ways long ago. He refused to elaborate, other than to say he had severed ties with that branch and had no intention of reuniting. The mention of that demon-blood lineage never escaped our lips, but I suspected he knew. There was a haunted glimmer in his eyes.

Glancing around, we spotted two small children running about, presumably his grandchildren. A handful of other family members hovered in doorways, eyeing us with mild suspicion. It felt like we'd stumbled into a real-life soap opera, with half the cast pretending ignorance. No matter how Karandeep probed or I gently insisted, the man wouldn't budge. He refused to take Poonam back or do anything about her. He just wanted to keep his hotel afloat, apparently on the brink of closure. So, with no better recourse, we left.

Walking back to the car, I mulled over the conversation. Another dead end, or maybe a piece in the puzzle. These folks definitely had demon blood somewhere in their lineage, but they refused to talk. Another rung in the ladder of cosmic madness. Karandeep must have noticed my quiet gloom because he patted my shoulder in a rare show of empathy.

We drove off, heading back to the agency, both of us lost in thought. The sky had begun to tinge with late-afternoon light, cars whizzing by. My phone buzzed with a message from the same unknown number that kept spamming me about budget updates for the demon-hunt. I ignored it. My mind was on Poonam and the half-lion monstrosities that had nearly devoured us last time.

Finally, we reached my apartment building in the government colony. Karandeep dropped me off, promising to check in later. I made my way upstairs, every muscle complaining from exhaustion. The day had drained me, physically and mentally.

My door was ajar. An immediate rush of adrenaline snapped me awake. The lock looked jimmied. Had some petty thief decided to rummage my place, or was something more sinister at play? Carefully, I nudged the door open and peered inside.

A figure crouched near my desk, rifling through drawers. He—or it—moved with unsettling stiffness, as though each joint were misaligned. Then he spun around, revealing a face that was half-decayed, eyes clouded with an unearthly glow. Another undead? In my apartment?

We locked gazes. For a heartbeat, neither of us moved. Then he lunged, trying to pin me against the wall. My agent reflexes took over. I twisted free, slamming him with a chair. He reeled back, but undead rarely feel pain the way we do. We scuffled across the living room, knocking over a lamp, scattering half my meager possessions. He grabbed for my throat, rancid breath hitting my face. I let out a furious growl, hooking a foot behind his leg to throw him off balance.

We crashed into the balcony door, the glass rattling ominously. The undead snapped at me with rotting teeth, drool flecking the floor. Summoning a desperate surge of strength, I yanked the door open, then hurled him outward. He clawed at me, leaving a ragged tear in my sleeve, but lost his grip. He tumbled over the railing with a dull, fleshy thud onto the courtyard below.

Panting, I stared down. The undead figure stirred, not quite dead—again?—so I dashed down the stairs in a half-frenzied rush to drag him back up. By the time I reached him, his limbs were twisted, but he still hissed in defiance. Another short struggle ensued. Eventually, I pinned him, improvised some rope from a neighbor's laundry line, and hauled him back to my flat, ignoring the shocked stares of a few residents. I slammed the door behind us.

Tying him to the sofa with trembling hands, I tried to interrogate him. "Who sent you? Why are you rummaging my place?" No response. He glared, lips twitching, but no words. Possibly because the spirit animating him had bailed. I tapped his chest, noticing a half-healed puncture. Another necro-puppet, no doubt.

Cursing under my breath, I pressed a hand to one of his open wounds, hoping to glean some clue from the residual energies. Big mistake. The moment my skin contacted undead flesh, an electric jolt hammered my system, like a psychic lash. My vision blurred, a roaring in my ears. Then I felt myself being yanked out of my body again, forcibly, painfully.

Everything dissolved into a swirl of white noise, my soul spinning somewhere beyond mortal confines. Then it stabilized, coalescing into another vision. The same ancient building, the same sense of ominous architecture. The demon insect creature stood there, time seemingly frozen. It turned its grotesque, half-human face toward me, as if waiting.

In a telepathic voice that rattled every nerve in my intangible form, it whispered, "Ah, finally you are here. I've been trying for quite some time."

## 11

### Big mistake. Big. Huge

Devrat had seen enough impossible things in his bizarre line of work that little could truly shock him anymore—or so he thought. Yet, as he now stood suspended in a whiteness beyond mortal comprehension, conversing with an insect demon that shaped the space around them, shock was the only apt word. He felt like a disembodied observer, drifting between existence and oblivion, forced to watch as the demon manipulated the limbo to show him some long-buried reality.

"Where… am I?" he asked feebly, his voice echoing in an emptiness that stretched infinitely in every direction. His arms felt weightless, or possibly nonexistent. If he hadn't been forcibly yanked here, he'd suspect he was dreaming.

"You stand between life and death," the demon said, voice entering Devrat's mind rather than his ears. "Some call it the Void. It's a no-man's-land of the spirit, a place to ruminate if one can stay conscious while severed from the mortal realm."

Devrat swallowed. "And… what am I doing here?"

"You, my dear friend, are special," came the telepathic reply. "Your repeated brushes with death—coupled with that cat fiasco, your soul reattachment, and the basement time dilation—have left your spirit unusually stable outside your body. Souls normally decay or dissipate, but you remain aware. I needed a mortal anchored thus to speak to me."

Devrat cleared his throat, fighting the swirl of vertigo. "Speak to you? You're a demon. Why do you need a human to talk to?"

The insect demon's mandibles twitched, as if in faint amusement. "My existence as a demon does not define me entirely. I need help, and ironically, you're in the best position to give it—if you so choose."

"How could I possibly help a demon?" he asked. "I've heard stories about you controlling a royal family, fathering half-demon heirs, and orchestrating murders. Why would I help you?"

A hiss reverberated through the whiteness, making the intangible ground ripple in protest. The demon's eyes glowed a subdued violet. "You speak of rumors, half-truths. Let me share my side. Perhaps you'll see that not all is as your agency claims."

"Fine," Devrat murmured, crossing phantom arms over his intangible chest. He tried to maintain a show of defiance, but it was difficult to be defiant when your body was half-energy in some cosmic waiting room.

The demon drifted sideways, the blank space shimmering in an array of hexagons and swirling shapes. "I was born at the crux of existence," it began. "We demons existed before mortal civilizations, formed from what you might call the shadows of creation. We fed on conflict, participated in cosmic battles. Then came the Great Separation, when realms parted and many of us were trapped in the mortal plane. Some thrived on corrupting humans. I, too, was among them."

A pang of sympathy flickered in Devrat's gut despite his better judgment. "So, you spent eons messing with humans?"

"Yes, until betrayal from my own kin left me broken, neither fully dead nor alive. My physical form disintegrated, but my consciousness lingered in agony. Over eons of drifting, I learned empathy. Pain does that. Eventually, I found enough strength to remake a small insect body. That's when Harish found me."

"Harish. The king?"

The demon nodded. "He recognized me for what I was, yet treated me kindly, never demanded boons. His family befriended me. In time, I reciprocated. They advanced on their own merits, but outsiders assumed *I* was orchestrating their success. Some saw me as an abomination and resolved to kill me. Others believed I was a boon from the gods. The family and I never forced illusions on them. We simply… coexisted."

A swirl of whiteness parted, revealing a frozen scene of an old hall where armed intruders confronted the king, who stood with anguish in his eyes, the demon at the threshold. Devrat recognized it from earlier visions. The demon turned to him. "Time is paused here. This is the final confrontation you glimpsed. You presumed I unleashed mass slaughter. But you must see what truly happened. Only by witnessing the outcome can you grasp the curse that now haunts my name."

Devrat steeled himself. He'd come expecting gore and betrayal. "Alright. Show me."

"Brace yourself," the demon said with a telepathic whisper of regret.

Time lurched into motion, and Devrat felt like a ghostly observer, floating behind the demon's shoulder. The intruders brandished swords, scowling at the king. "We know you harbor that demon," spat one man, presumably a local noble or rebellious retainer. The king pleaded with them to spare his friend, explaining that the demon meant no harm. The faction refused to listen. Tension soared.

Devrat expected the demon to lash out with supernatural force. Instead, the demon lifted its spindly arms in a posture of surrender. "I'll go peacefully if you do not harm this family," it said aloud, its voice sounding strangely gentle for a monstrous insect. The intruders exchanged wary glances. Some lowered their weapons in confusion.

But the king, in a tragic swirl of panic, lunged at the man who led the rebels—who also happened to be the king's own brother. They scuffled, swords clashing with dull clangs. In the chaos, the brother stabbed the king through the chest, the king's final words lost in a gurgle of blood. A hush fell over the hall. The intruders stood stunned at the murder they'd just committed. The brother stared at his fallen sibling, face twisted with horror and triumph rolled into one.

Devrat's spectral vantage quivered. He never expected the king's brother to be the killer. The demon made no move to rescue its friend, merely sank to its knees beside the dying monarch, gently cradling the body. The intruders were at a loss— some wanted to free the demon if it truly intended no harm, while others insisted it still had to die.

But the brother, spurred by power-lust or fear, seized the moment. He declared himself the new king, demanded the entire royal family who supported Harish be put to death, branding them traitors. The intruders, whipped into a frenzy, stormed the palace, forcibly rounding up men, women, and children. The demon remained in silent grief, letting itself be chained without resistance.

In short order, the demon was dragged to a large hall while the new king, incited by a cunning royal priest, decided they could *harvest* the demon's "magical properties" for themselves. Devrat watched in rising dread as a grotesque sacrificial ritual was prepared, with lines of chanting priests, and the demon shackled in the center. The demon spoke once to the new king, warning him that forcibly extracting demon essence would lead only to ruin. The king ignored it.

At a signal, the priests struck with knives, hacking the demon's body until blackish blood spilled across the stone floor. Devrat recoiled, heart hammering. This was an abomination. He expected the demon to fight back, but it refused. The final blow severed its head, yet still it lived, conscious enough to fix the new king with a final curse. The king and his loyal family members, in their greed, gathered around, performing an even more horrific act: they drank the demon's blood, then, under the priest's direction, carved up the demon's remains, distributing the pieces among themselves. Devrat wanted to retch at the cannibalistic spectacle. They believed consuming the demon would grant them immortality or unimaginable power.

Yet the demon, in its final telepathic breath, let out a bitter laugh, cursing them. A Shaashvat curse that bound their souls to eternal half-life. Devrat watched as the demon's final spark of life manifested in a swirl of dark energy that latched onto the new king's clan like an unholy tether.

The demon's voice whispered in Devrat's mind, narrating the aftermath: The curse gave them immortality, but not of flesh—their bodies could die, but their spirits remained restless. Over centuries, these cursed family members learned to possess fresh corpses, living a tortured existence bound to an endless cycle of dying and reanimating. Linked telepathically, they sensed each other's presence across distances. Factions emerged: some saw this as a vile horror they longed to end, others embraced it as a means to shape the world in their demon-laced image. Over time, these immortals scattered, forging secret empires, or fading into anonymity. And so the seeds of the undead clans rummaging through modern India were sown.

When the final vestiges of the demon's memory scene faded, Devrat found himself back in the white Void, trembling from the horrors he'd witnessed. The demon—somehow still present in this limbo—regarded him with an exhausted resignation.

"That is what they did to me," it said flatly. "I cursed them in my dying moment. A reflex, or perhaps an act of vengeance. I have lived with regret ever since."

Devrat could barely form words. "T-they… ate you? That is horrifying."

The demon's mandibles clicked softly. "Indeed. Yet that was centuries ago. Over time, some lineage members have come to regret their immortality, longing to break the curse. Others embrace it, forming undead factions. They now tear each other apart, each side misguided. The girl you call Poonam? She is of that bloodline, possibly the catalyst for igniting a final confrontation."

Breathing felt difficult in the void. "So… you want me to fix your cursed legacy? To bring about some closure?"

"I want… an end," the demon murmured. "To the curse and to my tortured existence. My spirit remains tethered to the mortal plane via the curse. I cannot rest. I've tried to appear many times, but my children's actions only spawn more violence. If you can help sever that link—undo the curse—I might finally know peace."

Devrat's mind whirled. He realized everything his agency believed might be half-truth. The demon was neither unrepentant nor an active puppet master. The actual puppet masters were the undead family, locked in a cycle of civil war. "I'll consider it," he whispered.

"Thank you," the demon said gravely. Then the swirl of whiteness shattered, and Devrat felt his consciousness snapped back into his battered mortal frame.

---

The battered Gurugram office felt emptier than usual. Karandeep leaned against a half-collapsed cubicle partition, phone pressed to his ear. On the other end was Vamsi, who had decided to revisit that suspicious transport company. Karandeep tried to caution him, but Vamsi was insistent.

"Something's off about those records," Vamsi repeated, voice echoing across static. "I see no real backgrounds for the employees. And the 'director' gave me half-baked files. I suspect they're part of that undead demon clan."

Before Karandeep could respond, he heard a shuffle of movement behind him. Turning, he found Poonam standing quietly, eyes distant. He forced a reassuring smile, ending the call with a promise to phone Vamsi soon. The girl asked about Devrat, about her granduncle, about why everything was so hush-hush. Karandeep improvised a comforting half-lie, describing how her granduncle "seemed happy" to hear about her, leaving out the old man's actual ambivalence. She grew unnervingly quiet, then left with a murmur about resting. Something about her posture suggested she knew more than she let on.

Left alone, Karandeep rummaged through old archives in an attempt to identify the monstrous lion-like creatures that had attacked them. He discovered references to Sunda and Upasunda, lesser demon lieutenants under some ancient demon rumored to have existed in epic times. Possibly that demon was the same insect demon controlling these abominations. The text ended ambiguously, implying the demon had "died," but never clarifying how. Typical. Karandeep shut the text, frustration mounting.

Then Devrat burst in, panting, sweat trickling down his temples. He looked half mad, stammering about how the demon had shown him the truth. "They— the royal family— they cut up the demon. They devoured him. That's how the curse started. The entire undead lineage is its twisted aftermath."

Karandeep stared at him, reeling from the brutality. "So the demon was the victim, not the perpetrator?"

Devrat nodded, dropping into a chair. "We had it all wrong. The demon cursed them at the moment of death. This is bigger than we realized. The entire undead clan traces back to that cursed bloodline."

Before Karandeep could process, a staffer barged in, breathless. "You asked for the girl, Poonam? She's… missing, sir. Gone."

Karandeep's heart sank. By the haunted look in Devrat's eyes, he knew they'd both realized the same thing: the cursed family might have just seized the one link that could unravel or finalize this entire fiasco.

---

Back at the transport company building, Vamsi reentered under the pretense of retrieving "missing documents." The entire place had a heightened tension. The reindeer sigil on a large plaque near the elevator now seemed glaringly ominous. No receptionist manned the front desk. Lights glowed from all floors—unusual for a late Saturday.

He took the stairs to the director's cabin, half-expecting an ambush. Sure enough, Bijay Mohan Mohanty sat behind his desk, flanked by the same older limp man and the tall, thin fellow. They stared at Vamsi as though they'd been waiting. The conversation was civil for about two minutes, culminating in Vamsi's request to interview some employees. Bijay obliged, summoning a timid woman named Sujata who claimed to know nothing. Vamsi noticed how she glanced nervously at Bijay for approval. Something was deeply off.

Midway through questioning, Vamsi's phone buzzed. Devrat was on the line, frantic, telling him the demon had just revealed a grotesque origin story for the undead. The entire clan might run its modern operations from this very office. Devrat warned: "Get the hell out before they corner you."

A cold sweat formed on Vamsi's brow. He ended the call with forced calm. "Thanks, Sujata," he said blandly. "That's all I needed."

Bijay's smile grew predatory. The older limp man rose, revealing a rotted face under the flicker of illusions, while the tall man's limbs twisted. The entire building was an undead nest.

Vamsi unleashed a short burst of protective energy from the old-lady spirit that hovered near him. The illusions wavered, revealing undead in the hallway. With no time to second-guess, Vamsi fled, the entire staff giving chase. Alarms or illusions triggered, the overhead lights blinking. He used spirit blasts to knock undead back, careening through cubicles, smashing a glass divider. It was half chase, half improvised warzone.

By sheer luck, he reached a side exit. More undead swarmed outside, but a passing truck nearly flattened one, letting Vamsi slip into a crowd of bystanders. He vanished among them, heart pounding, cursing the near disaster. If he'd stayed any longer, they might have forcibly turned him into a lifeless puppet. Gasping for breath, he searched for an auto rickshaw to go back to the office.

---

Panting, I gripped the edge of a half-toppled desk in the Gurugram office, trying to collect my thoughts. The demon's entire story replayed in my head: from its betrayal and near-death, to the tragic downfall of

King Harish, to the vile cannibalism that sealed the curse. I explained it all to Karandeep in a rush.

"So it was the *royal family* that truly murdered the demon, not the other way around," I said, throat dry. "In a twisted attempt to harvest its powers, they performed a sacrificial ritual, devouring the demon's flesh. That final act triggered the demon's dying curse, granting them immortality of the soul but cursing them with a restless existence. They can't die properly—once their bodies fail, their spirits linger, forcibly possessing new corpses if they want to remain active."

Karandeep looked sick. "That's… beyond horrifying. So these same cursed folks eventually branched out, forming factions, some wanting to end the curse, others seeing it as a twisted blessing. That lines up with our undead warring among themselves."

I nodded, rubbing my temples. "And Poonam's apparently part of that bloodline. One side wants to kill or capture her, the other might want to use her. Or she might be the key to breaking the curse entirely. The demon told me it just wants the curse undone so it can finally rest. Its spirit remains tethered to them somehow."

Karandeep exhaled. "But she's missing."

My stomach twisted. "We need to find her. They might have forcibly taken her, or she might have wandered off in confusion or under some mental pull. If we don't get her back, who knows what the warring undead might do."

A staffer rushed in, phone in hand. "S-sir, Vamsi's on the line. He escaped from that company building, but he says they're definitely all undead, and they know we're onto them."

I grabbed the phone, hearing Vamsi's ragged breathing. "You alright?"

"Barely. They almost pinned me. I'm safe for now, but we need a plan. They've definitely gone to ground or relocated. Next time they see me, it won't be so easy to slip away."

I swallowed. "We lost Poonam. She's missing from the office."

Vamsi cursed under his breath. "Then it's begun, Devrat. That clan is making moves. If they have the girl, they can do whatever they want—kill her, use her as leverage, or forcibly harness the demon's leftover powers."

I rubbed my sore shoulder. My body still felt new, as if reattached only days ago. "We'll figure out a way, Vamsi. We just need to track them. The demon says we might break the curse if we can gather certain relics or force the clan to sever the bond." I glanced at Karandeep, who nodded in grim agreement.

"Alright," Vamsi said quietly. "I'll regroup, meet you in Delhi by morning. Keep your phone on. We need to find the girl. This entire undead fiasco… it's about to blow up in our faces."

He ended the call. The staffer left us alone in the battered corridor. I leaned against the half-crumbled wall, trying to push back the wave of exhaustion. My mind reeled with the demon's horrifying final memory: the savage stabbing, the vile cannibalism, and that chilling moment when the demon's dying curse sealed their fate.

Karandeep cleared his throat. "So… we find Poonam, either talk sense into whichever faction has her, or forcibly get her out. Then maybe see if we can break the curse. With all the demon-lion creatures and undead around, that's a tall order. But maybe it's our only path."

I closed my eyes, picturing Poonam's innocent face, the traumatized girl who'd just begun to trust me. We had to save her, not just from the undead but from her own family's monstrous legacy. The demon had entrusted me with knowledge. If I turned my back on it, the curse would continue claiming innocent lives—or half-lives—for centuries more.

Outside, a wind rattled the debris in the hallway, as if echoing the tension coiling in my chest. I inhaled. "We'll do whatever it takes," I said softly. "We might be the only chance left for that demon—and for this cursed family. Let's see if that old bastard vantage-limbo power of mine can be put to good use after all."

Karandeep put a reassuring hand on my shoulder. "We'll find her. Let's go."

# 12

## Hasta la vista, baby

I don't recall ever feeling as dazed as I did the moment I learned Poonam was gone. For the first thirty seconds, I just stood in the corridor of the battered Gurugram office—though "office" might be a stretch, considering half the building had been scorched, the other half reeking of stale disinfectant from the recent undead invasion. My newly reattached human body still felt sluggish, my nerves raw from the soul-transfer procedure. Next to me, Karandeep hovered, arms folded, brow furrowed.

"How the hell did she leave?" I asked, my voice betraying my alarm.

A timid staffer—the same fellow who'd first delivered the news—shifted uneasily from one foot to the other.

"She—uh—we're not sure," he stammered. "She was here last night, but come morning, the room was empty. Door locked from the inside, window open. She's gone, sir."

My mind reeled. I'd last seen Poonam shortly after the fiasco in the basement, right after they'd forcibly reattached my soul to my battered body. She recognized me, even in my weakened state, and she'd comforted me as best a seven-year-old could. We parted ways—I'd assumed she was safe. Now she was missing. I wrestled with a swirl of panic and anger. The poor kid had been the focal point of so many monstrous forces—undead, demon-lion creatures, a cursed lineage. Possibly she'd been abducted.

"Did we check the cameras?" I demanded. The staffer nodded vigorously, scurrying off to rummage through half-functional CCTV feeds. Our security system was a joke on good days, especially after the infiltration. Still, we might catch a clue.

Karandeep exhaled, pressing two fingers to his temples. "Let's search. She might still be in the premises. So far, no one saw her leaving."

We parted ways, me ignoring the lingering soreness in my arms and legs. Staff joined the search, scouring storerooms, restrooms, even the rooftop where the lion-like creatures once rampaged. Others prowled outside, checking corners and supply truck parking. Tension rose with each passing minute.

Eventually, I reached her cabin, a small side room near the staff lounge that served as her makeshift living space. The door stood slightly ajar. Anxiety twisted in my gut as I pushed it open.

Inside, fluorescent overhead lights cast a clinical glow on a neat, minimal environment: a small bed, a battered desk, and a few children's knickknacks we'd salvaged. On the bed, sheets were folded neatly, as if she'd made her bed before leaving. My eyes drifted to the desk.

Some sweet wrappers littered one corner, likely from the snacks we'd given her. A small stack of drawings sat near a lamp—simple sketches of cartoons or random shapes. One depicted a large figure next to a smaller child with pigtails. I realized with a pang it might represent me, back when I was still out cold from the soul-transfer, or how she'd perceived me. Another drawing showed what seemed like a bright sun overshadowed by an insect-like silhouette in scribbly crayons.

Further rummaging turned up a couple of books about coping with trauma or finding happiness, presumably left by well-meaning staff. She'd dog-eared several pages, suggesting genuine interest. Finally, I found her clothes, folded meticulously in a small suitcase at the foot of the bed. The message was clear: she hadn't been snatched. She'd arranged her belongings and left of her own accord.

A jolt of frustration hammered me. She must have recalled something—maybe from her last conversation with Karandeep about her granduncle. We'd suspected a heritage hotel tied to her family's demon-lion fiasco. It all pointed there.

Moments later, Karandeep ambled in, breathless. "No sign of her outside," he said, voice grim. "Staff says the cameras were half-fried from last night's meltdown. Only one angle works. Looks like she slipped out around 4 A.M.—never triggered an alarm. She just… left."

I motioned to the tidy bed and neat belongings. "She left on her own," I concluded.

Karandeep nodded, jaw clenched. "I suspect so. Maybe our talk set things in motion. I told her about that hotel we found—her granduncle was there. I might've implied he was happy to see her, which was half-lie, half-truth."

I let out a weary sigh. "You told me earlier how strongly she reacted. So she decided to find him herself. Dammit."

Karandeep's shoulders slumped. "We should brief Anu."

We found Anu near the front corridor, directing staff to fix a broken door hinge. Hearing the news, she fumed—smacking a fist into a cracked plaster wall. "We're responsible for her safety! Now monstrous fiascos could erupt again."

After she calmed, we assembled a small search team. Meanwhile, a certainty gnawed at me: Poonam had gone to that heritage hotel we'd identified, likely walking into a final confrontation between two factions of her cursed family. My gut churned.

"We have to go there," I insisted. My words emerged in a shaky voice, my newly rejoined body still frail, but my determination unwavering.

Karandeep exhaled. "Let me gather a squad. We can't waltz in unprepared."

But I was done waiting. If Poonam truly walked into a demon-lion den, time was crucial. I recalled her tearful face, the sense that she might be used in some ritual sacrifice. My frustration with the usual bureaucratic dithering boiled over.

So, I resolved to go alone.

I told Karandeep I'd head out immediately. We had a battered agency sedan or maybe Karandeep's personal car. Let him gather backup and catch up. He frowned, rummaging for arguments. "You sure? You're still recovering from the soul reattachment. This is risky."

I squared my shoulders. "No choice. The more we delay, the greater the danger to her."

Anu overheard, scowling. She wanted a systematic approach. But my hunch felt rock-solid. Poonam was at that hotel, stepping into a final crisis. The best chance to save her was to arrive fast.

Karandeep reluctantly gave in, especially once a staffer mentioned Vamsi was off on a separate lead and wouldn't be back for hours. "All right. But you must be insane," Karandeep said. "Driving alone in your condition—"

I forced a grim half-smile. "I'll manage," I said, ignoring my lingering aches.

At near midnight, I hopped into Karandeep's battered hatchback. He left the keys in the ignition, sighing that it was likely a deathtrap for me, but better than waiting. My limbs still felt heavy, but I'd tested them enough to manage. Fine motor control was tough, but at least I was in my own flesh, no longer reliant on cat reflexes. I turned the ignition, letting adrenaline push me onward.

The drive felt surreal. The deserted roads lay silent under the moonlight. The city's bustle had vanished, replaced by the hush of empty streets. My mind roiled with tension, each passing minute ramping up my fear for Poonam. The battered car rattled, my heart pounded, but eventually I reached that heritage hotel on the outskirts. Tall gates, a small sign indicating closure at this hour. Dim lights flickered.

I parked in a side alley, scanning the premises. The place seemed half-dead. No sign of guests. I moved forward, letting my newly reacquainted legs carry me. My breathing quickened, noticing only a faint glow from within—some lamps left on.

I slipped through the main entrance, ironically unlocked. The reception was deserted, a single overhead bulb swaying. The odor of dust and faint incense clung to every surface. I recognized the same ancient paintings from prior visits—the swirling half-lotus symbol referencing her demon-lion lineage. One painting showed a temple I'd glimpsed in my dreams. Another pictured Sarbeswar himself, decades younger, labeled "Sarbeswar Mohanty."

"All this time it was here," I muttered, stepping through the gloom. "They're not even hiding."

Leaving reception, I followed a corridor into the main hall—dark, unoccupied, no sign of typical hotel operations. Light glowed beyond the building, so I drifted that way, eventually slipping out a side door into a courtyard.

A mild smoky scent wafted from somewhere in the yard. Creeping past manicured hedges, I spotted an outdoor fireplace near a rear garden. A circle of people sat around it, silhouettes outlined in flickering orange. My eyes adjusted. Sarbeswar perched on a low stool, clad in a dhoti and sweater, face drawn tight with exhaustion. Another half-dozen folks stood or sat around him in eerie silence.

I approached, tension knotting my stomach. They looked at me with calm expectancy, as though they'd known I'd come. Among them was Poonam, standing near a column, arms crossed. Even from afar, I saw the tracks of tears on her cheeks. My heart twisted. She'd come willingly, but she wasn't unhurt.

I stepped closer. The hush thickened. That's when I noticed two hulking shadows crouched on a low rooftop overhead—the lion-like creatures from the office attack. Their eyes glowed in the firelight, locked on me. A jolt of fear lanced through me. I remembered them nearly devouring me before my earlier brush with death.

"They won't do anything," Sarbeswar said softly. "Don't worry."

I forced a breath, voice trembling. "So they… work for you?"

Sarbeswar's expression remained neutral. "Yes. They guard us from the other faction. If you don't threaten us, they won't attack."

Anger boiled in me. "So you're the ones in conflict with your own family, unleashing demon-lion beasts, attacking our office, killing employees?"

Sarbeswar nodded without flinching. "That is correct, though you're oversimplifying. Let me clarify. We never wanted outside involvement, but events forced our hand. On the night of the attack, we tried not to harm your staff. Our creatures targeted the undead. Any staff fatalities came from the undead's actions, not us."

My mind reeled. "Highway ambush? The creature nearly swallowed me alive!"

He shrugged softly. "They're savage animals. Mistakes happen. We harbor no ill intent toward the agency. We just want to keep Poonam safe."

I shot a glance at the girl in the corner, silent, face etched with heartbreak. "If you wanted her safe, why not just keep her? That staged crime scene— why involve us?"

A faint, pained laugh escaped him. "We had to hide her from the other side. Letting your agency shelter her was strategic. She survived, didn't she?"

I clenched my fists. "So you used us. All those dead neighbors—staged?"

Sarbeswar lowered his gaze. "Yes. All staged. She's special, the apex of our bloodline. We needed her hidden until the time was right."

I seethed. "She's just a child. Doesn't that matter?"

His face tightened. "She's more than a child—she can end centuries of torment."

A chill sank into me. "End torment how? You plan to kill her?"

He gave a grim nod. "Yes, and ourselves. Only a final blood offering from the pure lineage can break the curse. Poonam's lineage merges all branches. This is the only way to sever our immortal suffering."

My rage flared. "That's madness! You trust some demon to end your curse if you slaughter yourselves? You'll just die."

A resigned shrug. "Better true death than living as rotting souls, trapped in undead cycles. We tried everything—mass suicide, labs in the Andamans— no success. A demon told us: one last path. Poonam's blood, plus ours, so the demon can break the curse."

Desperation choked me. "We can help you. The agency might figure something out—"

Sarbeswar laughed mirthlessly. "We approached your agency decades ago. They didn't believe or care enough to solve it. We're done waiting."

I hissed, stepping forward. "I won't let you do this."

He shrugged again. "It's begun. By dawn, we'll all be dead, the curse undone. A gamble, but our best shot."

I tried to rush for Poonam. Watchers pinned my arms, holding me. She walked over, eyes glistening. Kneeling, she hugged me. "I'm sorry," she whispered. "I wanted to run, but I can't escape it. I have to do this."

I struggled, but her small hand patted mine. "Thank you for everything," she said softly. Then she left through the back door, escorted by family. My watchers eventually released me as something else drew their attention. A hush fell. A new presence arrived from the front.

Looking up, I saw a horde of undead at the hotel entrance—led by Bijay in a neat suit, hair immaculate. Rows of rotting corpses glowed with unholy sparks in their eyes. Sarbeswar exhaled, telling me quietly, "They found us."

From the rooftop, the lion-things snarled, bristling for a fight. The watchers parted, warily. A three-way confrontation formed: Sarbeswar's clan wanting to finish the ritual, the undead wanting to stop or exploit them, and me, alone with no illusions of heroism.

"They can kill us, but it won't matter," Sarbeswar said, rising from the fire. "We're ready to die anyway. Let me try one last talk with them."

He walked forward, lion-beasts flanking him. Bijay strode from the undead, half-smiling. "Hello, Uncle. Last time I saw you, I was twenty."

Sarbeswar sighed. "I'm glad you're here, ironically. We can end this, our suffering is done tonight."

Bijay scoffed. "Suffering? We built an empire with immortality. We can shape the world. You want to throw that away for a worthless sacrifice."

Before Sarbeswar replied, agency vehicles roared up, tires crunching gravel. Karandeep, Vamsi, and a handful of agents emerged with weapons or magical artifacts. Maybe a dozen, not enough for a massive undead fight, but hopefully enough. Vamsi shouted:

"Both parties, stand down! We know your motives. You won't complete your ritual or continue these undead raids."

A hush. Sarbeswar, Bijay, lion-beasts froze in a tense standoff. Sarbeswar turned to Bijay:

"Step down, nephew. Let me and my people do what we must. We can't keep living this half-life."

Bijay's eyes flashed. "Your mania ends now." He lunged with supernatural force, punching Sarbeswar's chest. Bones cracked. Sarbeswar collapsed, presumably dead.

**Chaos** erupted. "ATTACK!" Bijay bellowed, ordering the undead forward. The lion-things roared, pouncing. Agents fired spells, watchers scrambled. The courtyard became a battlefield— shrieks, roars, muzzle flashes, arcs of spiritual energy. A car revved among the undead, driven by a wild-eyed man. He nearly ran me down. I dove aside. A lion-thing jumped onto the hood, trying to break the windshield. Undead battered it with rods, impaling it. The creature roared in agony.

I glimpsed Karandeep amid the fray, fists flying. Vamsi crouched behind an overturned table, presumably conferring with his protective spirit, launching blasts that pinned undead. Some watchers tried to hold their ground. It was a swirl of dust, shrieks, and lashing limbs.

Desperate to find Poonam, I forced my way inside the hotel. Karandeep was blocked by more undead, so I pressed on alone. The corridor was dim, an emergency lamp flickering. I heard faint echoes of the battle.

Suddenly, Bijay emerged from the shadows, hair still pristine despite a bleeding brow. He sneered:

"You again. If not for you, I'd have reached the roof in time to stop this nonsense."

I braced. He lunged. Even weakened, I fought back. He pinned me, I twisted free. We exchanged savage blows. Finally, I toppled a heavy cabinet onto him. He tumbled down a short flight of stairs, pinned. For the moment, he was out.

Panting, I continued upstairs, heart pounding with the dread that Poonam was on the roof, about to die.

At the rooftop access door, I shoved it open. The night air slapped me. A single lamp cast a pallid glow. Then my blood ran cold: Poonam lay on the floor, a dagger in her abdomen. Two older women from the family also lay dead, blood pooling. My mind recoiled.

She was gone. I dropped to my knees beside her, pressing a trembling hand to her cheek. "No," I whispered. "No." No immediate sign of a struggle—she must have willingly participated in a final ritual.

Footsteps thundered behind me—Bijay, or some undead. Indeed, Bijay staggered in, arm bleeding, face twisted with fury. He spotted Poonam's corpse.

"They did it? Without me?" Confusion warred with anger. He glowered at me, eyes blazing:

"If not for you," he snarled, "I could've saved her, or used her. Now everything's lost!"

He grabbed me, slamming me into a wall. I gasped, dizziness clouding my vision. "I'll kill you for delaying me," he hissed, choking me. My mind reeled with desperation. Then I spotted an open wound on his shoulder, raw and weeping. If I repeated that weird soul-manipulation trick from prior fiascos, maybe I could do something. I pressed my hand to the wound, focusing on forcibly yanking my soul into the void.

Abrupt blankness. No color, no wind—just a white hush. I recognized the limbo realm. I stumbled, calling for Poonam. She'd died minutes ago, so maybe her spirit hovered here. Then I saw her figure in the distance, wearing the same clothes, face etched with sorrow.

"Devrat," she whispered, as I approached. She tried to hug me, but our forms passed through each other in intangible half-light.

"How did you get here?" she asked softly.

"Doesn't matter," I said. "We have to—" I halted, noticing another presence: a strikingly handsome man standing calmly, as if waiting.

He turned, noticing me. "Interesting," he said. "Who are you to enter this in-between realm so freely?"

I glared. "Are you the demon they summoned to break the curse?"

He gave a faint chuckle. "In a sense. I made a contract with them. Your presence changes nothing. How'd you forcibly yank your soul out mid-fight?"

"Never mind," I snapped. "You can't condemn Poonam's soul to oblivion. She doesn't deserve that."

He blinked. "I'm not condemning her. My deal is that they kill themselves, I sever their curse. Freed from immortality, they rest. Meanwhile, I get to return to mortal existence. Poonam was the key. She's died, so presumably the ritual is complete, or nearly."

A swirl parted, revealing the **insect creature** from my visions—chitinous limbs, compound eyes. It hissed:

"You two bicker too loudly. The final stage proceeds in the mortal realm; this is just the aftershock."

I recognized it from centuries-old dreamlike recollections. "You're that demon from the temple fiasco," I murmured.

It nodded. "Once forced to be a demon. Now I watch humans. The family that devoured part of me centuries ago triggered this curse. This new demon man has a separate arrangement to end it. The cost is high."

I turned to the handsome man. "What's your real gain? You resurrect on Earth, reaping their souls?"

He shrugged. "Basically, yes. They want out. I want in. Everyone wins, except Poonam, but she was always fated to die. Her lineage ties all branches."

I clenched my jaw. "Let her soul go. She's innocent."

He studied me. "I can do that. I can't resurrect her body, but I can free her spirit from the family's nether. She can pass on."

Relief flared in me. "Then do it."

He nodded. "I will. In return, I want a host for my rebirth. Possibly through you or your lineage. You meddled, so now I might choose your future child as my mortal vessel. Could be interesting."

Horror shot through me. "My child? But I'm not—"

He laughed gently. "Give it time. Meanwhile, you get Poonam's freedom. A fair trade."

Before I could protest, he vanished in swirling lights. The insect creature bowed:

"We parted ways once, agent. My business here is done. Farewell."

It dissolved, leaving only Poonam, tears shimmering. "Thank you," she said. "I guess I'm free now—no more curse."

I tried to embrace her intangible form. "I'm sorry," I whispered. "I tried to save you."

She shook her head. "It's okay. We had some good moments, right?"

A flicker of a smile. Then the realm trembled, swirling lights devouring the scene. I shouted, but it all vanished.

Abruptly, I was back in my battered human form in the hotel's top-floor corridor. Bijay choked me, but his eyes bulged, blood trickling from every orifice. He dropped me, stumbling. The undead minions collapsed one by one, souls liberated from immortal shackles. The entire cursed network unraveled. Bijay gurgled, trying to speak, then fell dead.

Stunned, I recovered my breath, scanning the hallway. Bodies everywhere—some watchers, some undead. No movement. The curse, undone.

I rushed to Poonam's side. She was truly gone. Her body, a dagger wound in the abdomen. Yet I felt a faint solace recalling how the demon promised to free her spirit.

In a daze, I scooped up Poonam's body, ignoring my own exhaustion, staggering down the stairs. The building reeked of death and dust. Outside, the yard lay strewn with corpses—undead, watchers, at least one lion-thing riddled with spears. Another might have fled.

Karandeep emerged from behind a wrecked sedan, a gash on his forehead. He spotted me with Poonam's body, face falling. "Oh, God."

I nodded. The confrontation ended, no more roars or shrieks. Agents, battered, combed the grounds. Some still-living family members cradled children. Freed from the curse at last.

Anu and Vamsi conferred by a parked staff car, forming a makeshift perimeter. Karandeep ushered me to a medical vehicle. Gently, I laid Poonam's form inside, tears pricking my eyes.

"It's over, right?" Karandeep asked in a hushed tone, stepping next to me.

I stared at Poonam's face, heartbreak pounding in my chest. "Yeah," I whispered. "It's over."

Agents rummaged for evidence among the corpses. Surviving children were guided to an ambulance. Freed from centuries of soul-bond torment, they could lead normal lives. A few older relatives, undone by the severed link, lay catatonic.

Anu approached, face set with grim exhaustion. "Lot of dead. We'll drown in paperwork again."

Karandeep offered a hollow laugh, patting my arm. "At least the nightmares might stop."

I stared at Poonam's pale features. My mind echoed with the demon's final vow—this mess might be over. But for now, heartbreak trumped everything.

## 13

### Frankly, my dear, I don't give a damn

I never thought I'd see the Gurugram office fully repaired—and certainly not so soon after the carnage we faced. Yet here I was, padding through the freshly painted corridors, marvelling at walls that no longer bore scorch marks or deep claw scratches. The new tile floors gleamed under overhead lights, and the faint smell of drying paint mingled with the aroma of samosas. It was surreal, this clash between bureaucratic normalcy and the memory of demon-lion attacks still haunting my mind.

At the front lobby, the staff had set up a little "Return to Office" party. Plastic chairs were arranged in neat rows, a flimsy fold-out table laden with cake and chips, along with a few bottles of soda. Colorful streamers drooped from the ceiling, halfhearted attempts at festivity. Scattered conversation and forced laughter filled the air. Clearly, no one had forgotten that seven staffers died here not so long ago, or that we nearly lost the entire building to undead infiltration. But if there's one thing the agency is good at, it's forging normalcy from the ashes of chaos.

Karandeep and I made our way past the table, ignoring the half-melted icing on a large rectangular cake that read "Welcome Back." He carried a sheaf of documents under one arm. I still wasn't entirely used to my newly reattached human body—my last recollection had me in a cat's frame—but I was recovering. The soul reattachment surgery was successful, they said. Probably cost the agency a fortune in clandestine necromancy budgets. I still felt a phantom ache in my chest, though, as if my body recognized it had died twice (or thrice?) and refused to settle entirely.

"We have to see Anu," Karandeep reminded me, tapping the folder he held. "She wants the final incident report."

I nodded, letting him lead the way. The festive chatter receded as we navigated deeper into the building, passing a handful of staff who waved politely. Some still gave me wide-eyed stares— death and resurrection tend to garner attention, even in a department that handles supernatural fiascos daily. At last, we reached Anu's cabin, its door half- ajar. The new sign on it read "Regional Head Office: Ms. A. Dsouza," the paint barely dry.

Inside, the office felt oddly calm. A large wooden desk stood at the center, lined with stacks of paperwork, and behind it, Anu—our short, no- nonsense department head—sat flipping through a thick folder, lips pursed. She wore a crisp blouse and her hair was pulled back in a tight bun. At the corner of her desk, a half-eaten pastry sat neglected on a paper plate, presumably from the mini-party.

Karandeep coughed. "Ma'am, we have the report."

Anu gestured us to chairs. "Sit." Then she resumed reading, occasionally glancing up over her wire-rimmed glasses. I took the seat on the left, Karandeep on the right. The moment I settled, a faint wave of gratitude stirred in me—just being able to bend knees, elbows, and ankles properly again felt like a blessing. No more cat limbs, no more precarious leaps to door handles.

We waited in silence for a minute while she skimmed. Samosa crumbs dotted her desk, and from the corridor we could hear the muffled hum of staff making small talk about the new paint job.

"All right," Anu said at last, flipping a final page. "So this is your official account of the… fiasco. The culminating incident with those undead factions, the demon-lion creatures, the cursed bloodline, and the child's death."

Her tone was neutral, but I noticed the flicker of genuine fatigue in her eyes. She'd lost staff, faced a PR nightmare, and had to orchestrate a massive hush-up operation. Seven employees died, plus the countless bodies at that heritage hotel fiasco. Even for a department that deals with the paranormal, that was a lot.

I cleared my throat. "Yeah, it's all in there. We included details on each group, the curses, the final confrontation."

She nodded slowly, shifting her gaze. "Occasionally, I might ask clarifications." She thumbed back a page. "For instance, here on page eight, you mention the infiltration at the hotel was a 'three-way battle.' Did you truly confirm that none of the staff from the father's side—uh, Sarbeswar's side—initiated the assault on your men?"

Karandeep and I exchanged glances. He shrugged. "From what we saw, they were locked in conflict with the undead. Our folks were caught in the crossfire."

I chipped in with a half-sarcastic snort. "They basically had lion-lion creatures that might've taken swipes at us. So yes, it's complicated. But the real impetus was from the undead side. They triggered open hostilities."

Anu tapped her pen. "So complicated. Another embarrassment for us, on top of the prior fiasco." Her voice tightened. "Not to mention the astronomical number of dead people, many of whom had questionable legal identities. We're dealing with a mess behind the scenes."

Karandeep gave an uneasy laugh. "How are we spinning that, exactly? A massive gas leak? Flooding? People with bullet holes and claw marks—doesn't that raise eyebrows?"

Anu exhaled, rubbing her temples. "A public relations firm is on it, plus a group of specialized psychologists. We're telling local officials it was a chemical spill that caused rapid necrosis, plus hallucinations among the survivors. Typical cover. Takes a lot of carefully placed hush money."

I sighed. "It's insane how we can bury this so easily."

She snapped the folder shut. "Well, you did a thorough job in the field. The final resolution— whatever it was—put an end to the curse. We can breathe again. So… good work." Her words came out forced, but I heard the undercurrent of grudging respect.

She eyed me pointedly. "Devrat, in particular, you've done a splendid job. Surviving that cat fiasco, pushing through two or three near-death experiences… That's something. I have a piece of news for you."

I blinked. "News?"

A faint smile tugged at her lips. "You're being promoted."

A hush fell. I hadn't expected that. Usually, the agency overlooked me in favor of golden boys like Vamsi. My heart stuttered. Karandeep broke the silence with a grin, patting me on the shoulder. "He's too speechless to say thank you. I'll do it for him. Thank you, Anu."

Anu gave a curt nod. "You earned it. This last week was one of the worst in my entire tenure here—mass casualties, demon threats, and so forth. But at least it's over. We're back on track, or so it seems." She paused, flipping a separate sheet. "We also have the overtime records. Considering Devrat died multiple times—"

"Three," I interjected dryly.

"Three times," Anu corrected, rolling her eyes. "We're awarding you and Karandeep some hefty compensation. Here." She extended two envelopes. Karandeep took them, handing me mine. Inside lay official letters plus a small slip indicating a bonus deposit. A part of me warmed—financial relief from all this madness.

"And," Anu added, "you're both eligible for five days of paid vacation. Use it wisely. If you want more, talk to finance. But I can't guarantee more than that."

I nodded, trying to form a coherent "thank you." A swirl of complicated emotion twisted in my chest: we lost so many. The child I tried to protect died anyway. And yet, a promotion and a pay bump felt… undeservedly comforting. But I was too drained to argue. "I appreciate it," I managed softly.

Karandeep inhaled. "What about the kids who survived the meltdown from that cursed family? The orphans?"

Anu folded her arms. "We took them in. They appear free from the curse—completely. They're normal children now, or so our tests indicate. We're seeking a caretaker or an adoption channel. Their entire extended family line is basically wiped out." She grimaced. "It's a grim situation, but at least they can have normal lives."

I nodded, relieved at that small mercy. My mind flickered to Poonam. She never got that second chance.

As if reading my thoughts, Anu turned grave. "We also handled Poonam's funeral. With all the security concerns, we couldn't let you attend. But rest assured, it was done with full respect. I know you cared."

A lump rose in my throat. "Thank you," I murmured.

She tapped a pen on her desk. "Which brings me to one final question: we can't fully parse how the curse ended that night. Was it pure happenstance that the entire undead faction and the watchers' side simultaneously collapsed?"

I shifted uncomfortably. "It's all in the report. I don't have further insights. Possibly they completed a destructive ritual or some demon backfired. I was on the roof. Everything ended abruptly."

Anu's lips tightened. "We know you were there, physically. Are you certain you have no further recollection?"

I held her gaze. The events in that limbo plane, the demon's bargain, Poonam's final ephemeral presence—I had zero intention of sharing that. "I sincerely don't know," I lied, or half-lied. "One moment it was chaos, next moment it was over. I can't unravel it better than that."

Anu glared, then relented. "Fine. If you recall anything, you let me know." She gestured us away. "Now go. I have a desk's worth of fiasco to tidy."

We left the cabin. I clutched my envelope, mind still swirling with the contradictory swirl of promotion and gloom. Karandeep parted ways at a side corridor, patting me on the back. "I'm heading out early. My wife's waiting. See you tomorrow?"

"Sure," I said. He gave a last wave and vanished, leaving me in a maze of staffers. I ambled to my old desk—freshly reassembled and relocated to a corner near a new potted plant. The moment I approached, I spotted Vamsi rummaging in the drawers. He wore bandages around his head, an arm in a cast, but still exuded that calm competence I'd grudgingly admired.

He turned at the sound of my footsteps, offering a crooked grin. "Hey, Devrat. Just checking if you stole my pen." He raised his uninjured arm, showing a battered ballpoint. "Found it."

I smiled wryly. "I wasn't aware I was a pen thief. Good to see you upright. Heard you took quite a beating at that final confrontation."

He chuckled, leaning on my desk. "That's standard, right? The job never spares us. Anyway, want to step outside for a chat?"

I nodded. We drifted out a side exit where the new paint smell wasn't so overpowering. A small bench faced a half-finished garden patch. He sank onto it with a groan, rotating his stiff shoulders.

"So," he said quietly, "I'm being transferred to Meghalaya soon. Heard rumors about a Mande Barung sighting. Another cryptid fiasco. Could be fun."

I nodded, tension in my chest. "You sure you're well enough to jump to another crisis?"

He shrugged. "That's the job. They want me to handle it. Meanwhile, I hear you're… continuing here, or maybe some new role. Congratulations on the promotion."

"Thanks," I said, fiddling with the band of my watch. "I guess."

His gaze sharpened. "Hey, real talk. That final night with the cursed family—did you do something? The official line is hazy. The soul-liberation or demon-lion meltdown all happened in an instant. The kill ratio was insane."

I exhaled, my mind going back to the deal with that demon in limbo. "I can't answer, Vamsi. Not because I don't trust you, but because… I genuinely can't talk about it. Let's say it ended. The curse is gone."

He studied me, brow furrowed. "You didn't let a demon out in the world, right? Some unstoppable force?"

I forced a half-laugh. "No. Don't worry." That was a partial truth. The demon insisted it would be born into the mortal realm eventually, though. Not quite rampaging from day one.

Vamsi stared at the horizon, the half-constructed building across the street. "All right. I'll take your word for it." He rummaged for his phone. "By the way, do you have a cat? There's one in the parking lot that keeps giving me the creeps. Ugly brown thing, stares at me like it wants to share secrets."

A flick of dread twisted in me. I recalled the catlike form that might have survived—the second lion creature or something. Or maybe it was something else. Pasting a casual smile, I forced a shrug. "Um, yeah, I adopted a stray. She's harmless."

Vamsi shrugged. "Suit yourself. I'll pass. Ugly cat." He patted my shoulder lightly with his uninjured hand. "Anyway, Devrat, good luck. This department, this job… it's crazy. People like you keep it afloat."

I swallowed the lumps of unspoken truths. "Thanks, Vamsi. Safe travels."

He made his way toward the lot. I, too, headed that direction after a moment. Even from the distance, I spotted a familiar brown cat perched on the hood of my battered sedan, eyes glowing faintly. I exhaled. So it survived—the creature that had presumably escaped the final meltdown, or the demon's lesser minion.

I approached the car, scanning for onlookers. The cat hopped down, regarding me with an unsettling intelligence. I stepped close, voice low. "You. I never buried your body, so I guess you used it as a host?"

The cat stared with calm. Then, in a quiet telepathic hush that pressed against my mind, it answered, "Yes. You have enough attachment to this cat's remains that it serves as a stable vessel. It suits me well."

I suppressed a shudder. So one of the shape-shifting creatures, or a demon-ling entity, now wore the cat's form. "Why are you here?"

The cat flicked its tail. "A promise is a promise. My Master—the demon who ended the curse—intends to be reborn in your lineage. I stay to ensure no interference. You're to become the father of that demon's mortal vessel."

My blood ran cold. "That's ridiculous. I can refuse to have kids. Or I can kill it at birth."

The cat's ear twitched. "We have ways to ensure you conceive a child. And if it's a daughter, that's fine, my Master might prefer a female host. You can't outrun cosmic bargains."

Rage simmered. "So I'm stuck with you lurking around, ensuring the demon is born to me. This is insane."

The cat let out a purr-like chuckle. "Insane, but sealed in blood. And you aided it, remember? The demon freed Poonam's soul. This is the cost."

Weariness weighed on me. "Fine," I muttered, opening my car door. The cat hopped in the back seat. "But don't expect me to cooperate easily."

"We shall see," it replied, settling on the worn upholstery.

I turned the ignition, pulling away from the office's celebratory chaos. My mind churned with a thousand anxieties—a demon child in my future, the memory of Poonam's final smile, the overshadowing sorrow of near-constant death. But for the moment, I needed a break.

I took a detour to a local salon, stepping in with bandages half-hidden under my shirt. The cat strolled after me, drawing perplexed stares from staff. I wanted a haircut, a minor attempt at feeling normal. As the barber trimmed my hair, the cat perched on a side chair, blinking. They found it odd, but I waved it off as "my emotional support pet."

Afterward, I swung past the heritage hotel site, half-lifted security tape fluttering in the wind. Agency trucks were presumably done clearing the scene. A handful of workers hammered boards over broken windows. The place looked like a ghost—all silent, with a sign out front referencing a gas leak as the official cause of multiple fatalities. A crane was removing the large name board from the facade. The entire bloodline had perished or gone into some deep amnesia, no longer cursed. Another chapter closed, ephemeral as a dream.

Late evening found me driving toward Meerut, my hometown. Over phone calls, my mother insisted on my presence—they'd scheduled a meeting with the prospective bride's family. I wanted to bail, my heart too raw from the job's horrors. But my parents persisted, thrilled at the possibility I'd settle into a normal married life. Ignorant of the demon child fiasco looming overhead, obviously.

I pulled up to my parents' modest house in a quiet lane. The cat hopped out, ignoring my attempt to keep it hidden. My father, an ex-engineer in his sixties, stepped onto the porch, arms folded. He was tall, balding, ex-military posture. My mother, a retired teacher with a warm smile, bustled forward. Their eyes lit up upon seeing me, then flicked to the cat.

"What is that creature, Devrat?" Mother asked.

"An adopted stray," I said tersely, hoping they wouldn't pry.

They welcomed me inside. After a quick dinner, they reminded me we had to "go see the girl" tomorrow. They had arranged a meeting that very morning—a typical Indian matchmaking session. My father was beaming with paternal pride. My mother fussed over my hair (just trimmed) and asked why I was so pale. I let them believe it was from stress at the "government job." They barely grasped the supernatural dimension I lived in. If I tried to explain demon-lion beasts, they'd assume I was reciting a ghost story.

The next morning, we readied ourselves. The cat hung around quietly, an unsettling presence. My mother eyed it suspiciously but said nothing, perhaps deciding not to spoil the mood. We drove in my father's battered SUV across town to the bride's house. A typical two-story family home in a residential area, complete with bright marigold creepers along the walls and a rangoli pattern at the threshold.

We were greeted warmly by the girl's parents, who ushered us into a living room with plastic-covered sofas and a table set with sweets. The usual small talk ensued: her parents praising Ishita's talents in writing, my parents bragging about my stable government position. None of them had a clue about the real nature of my agency's work. For them, "government job" equaled "respectable," plus stability.

Eventually, Ishita stepped in—a tall, slender woman in a simple salwar kameez, hair pinned back. She looked average, but something about her easy smile and bright eyes stirred a flutter in my chest. I felt awkward, having come fresh from demon curses and cat transformations. She sat politely, greeting me. Then my mother proposed we speak alone.

We ascended a short flight of stairs to the rooftop. A gentle breeze drifted by as we stood near a half-finished storeroom. Ishita spoke first, asking about my job. I tried to downplay it, saying I worked in a niche government department dealing with "special cases." She found it intriguing, especially since she was a writer dabbling in ghost stories and occult themes. That caught me off guard—someone comfortable with the bizarre?

She laughed lightly. "I publish them under a pseudonym. My parents think I do children's books."

I let out a genuine chuckle, feeling a flicker of relief. "I guess we both have hidden sides to our work."

We stood there awkwardly, exchanging small talk about the city, our parents, the typical forced banter of an arranged meeting. Yet she had a sincerity in her voice that I found reassuring. I started feeling that maybe—just maybe—there was a chance for normalcy. Then, out of the corner of my eye, I spotted a familiar figure in the shadow of the storeroom door.

Poonam.

She stood, wearing a white dress, intangible, an otherworldly glow about her. My breath caught, heart pounding. The last time I saw her in the mortal realm, she was dead on a rooftop. Now her spirit shimmered before me, an echo in the living world.

"I was wondering when you'd show up," I breathed, stepping aside. Ishita frowned, "What?" as I turned away from her.

Poonam gave me a gentle smile. "I decided to stay. I can be your protective spirit, maybe. You gave me a second life in a sense. I don't want to drift away."

Tears stung my eyes. "I'm so glad," I whispered. "I thought I lost you forever."

She bowed her head. "I'm not fully here. But I can anchor to your aura, help you in your job. Or just… exist with you, if that's okay."

Ishita coughed behind me, confusion etched on her face. I realized I'd spoken aloud. I turned, stammering, "Uh… sorry, I…." She blinked. "You see her too?" she said in a small voice.

My eyes widened. "Wait, you can— you can see Poonam?"

Ishita exhaled, relief and fear mixing on her features. "I thought I was the only one who saw ghosts. I… I always had that ability, seeing apparitions or spirits. I was dreading your reaction if I told you."

My mind spun. A sense of awe overcame me. So Ishita also perceived the supernatural plainly, possibly more so than my oblivious parents. She'd presumably noticed Poonam's ghost creeping in the shadows. The two of them stared at each other, uncertain but not hostile.

"She's not going to hurt you," I said softly. "She's… a friend. A lost child who found a second existence as a spirit."

Ishita nodded, lips trembling. "I can sense she means no harm. I was just terrified you'd call me insane if I told you I see her."

A wave of warmth filled me. The improbable coincidences of my life never ceased. "No, I—well, you're talking to the perfect person for that secret." I managed a crooked grin. "Are you sure you're okay with all this, though?"

She stared at me with earnest eyes. "I was worried you'd reject *me* for seeing ghosts. But it seems like you live with them daily."

Poonam hovered near, an amused twinkle in her translucent eyes. "I guess it's sorted out," she teased. I teased a smile.

"So are you okay, you think we can talk?" Ishita asked with caution. I can sense the apprehension in her eyes.

I looked at her for a second, flipping back to Poonam for a second. For a person with some terrible luck, this feels like a different situation than I was used to.

"Yeah, I think we can talk".